Love, Lessons, Lies, and the Game of Life

Book 1:

The Beginning

by Dr. Charmaine Marie, Ed.D.

Published by: Real LOVE Publications

Love, Lessons, Lies, and the Game of Life

Book 1:

The Beginning

by Dr. Charmaine Marie, Ed.D.

Copyright © 2025 by: Real LOVE Publications.

ISBN#: 978-1-7377075-8-5

Printed in the United States of America

Thank you for taking time out to read,

Love, Lessons, Lies, and the Game of Life

Book 1:

The Beginning

We hope you enjoy the book.

Please do a book review on Amazon.com

to let us know what you think.

Prologue

I'm Marie Tucker, the woman who has two men. Yeah, you heard that right. Marcellus? He's been my heart since I was 16. Back then, it was puppy love, innocent, sweet, and dreamy. But now? It's the kind of love people write songs about. Real, unconditional, forever kind of love. The kind of love that makes you think destiny had a hand in it. He's my king, my first, and my always.

And then there's Dupree. Now, he was different. I met him on some "don't mess with me" energy. He was supposed to be a one-night deal, my little revenge story. But let me tell you, one night turned into the most unforgettable night of my life. Fun, fire, and the kind of conversation that stays with you. Dupree brought that gangster love into my life when I was 23, and somehow, he turned it into real, unconditional love, too. He's my other king, and guess what? He's forever, too.

I know what you're thinking. "This chick's crazy, right?" Nah, this isn't crazy. It's real. I love them both, and they love me. Not just love, though, they adore me. These two kings would move heaven and earth for me, and I'd do the same for them.

I've seen the boys, the players, and the wannabes. Marcellus and Dupree have seen the same. One day, we all woke up and said, "Why waste time on the outside world when we could build our own empire?" So, we did just that. Now we run businesses, stack wealth, and live like the legends we are.

We're the Tuckers. Yes, I always use my name, because I'm that woman. The kind of woman men don't just want, they need. Everything about me screams power, loyalty, and love. And trust me, no one could treat them better than I do. Out there? There's nothing but chaos and hate. We know because we've lived it. But in here? With Us? It's nothing but peace, prosperity, and pure happiness. We've built a world where joy is the only standard, and no one, not a single soul can take that from us.

This is our life. Our love. Our legacy. And we're unstoppable.

Life is a journey, and if you're here, buckle up because this ride isn't for the faint of heart. I'm going to take you on a trip, a raw, unfiltered journey through love, life, heartbreak, triumph, and all the chaos in between. Before we dive in, let me give you a heads-up: I'm firm in my approach, but I'm also full of love. I don't play games, though I know how to have fun. I never back down, and trust me, I've had to fight for the life I live now.

This book isn't just a story; it's an experience. We're going to go back to the beginning. I'll narrate here and there to give you the depth you need to feel every moment with me, because there's a lot to unpack. You'll see where I started, where I've been, and how I got to where I am now. There might be some back and forth because I will tell you how I remember it.

Let me warn you, though: my life wasn't some picture-perfect fairytale. It was messy, complicated, and full of twists and turns. Everything was supposed to be mapped out. My parents created greatness, starting from the bottom, that I could have just walked into, but I made my choices, right or wrong, and I'm standing in the life I've built because of them.

You'll meet my first loves, my best friends, and yes, my kings, who are now my two lifelong partners. But before you think you've got me figured out, remember this: I've had my share of "in-betweeners." Oh, those in-betweeners, they taught me lessons I never asked for but absolutely needed.

This isn't just a love story or a drama. It's real life, my life. I want you to feel every laugh, every tear, every tough decision, and every moment of joy. There's no sugar-coating here, no fluff. Just me, raw and unfiltered.

So, stay tuned. This isn't just my story; it's a joy ride into the life of my life.

Chapter One: 1988 The Beginning

Marie was a standout in every way. A bright, ambitious young lady, she excelled both in and out of the classroom. An honor roll student and the president of the student council at Benson High School, Marie was known for her infectious personality and ability to light up any room. Her smooth brown skin, shoulder-length bobbed hair, and a unique heart-shaped mole under her eye made her unmistakable. Standing at 5 feet 3 inches and weighing about 120 pounds, Marie carried herself with confidence, her distinct bow-legged walk adding to her charm. A social butterfly through and through, she loved talking to people and sharing a good laugh.

Marie's mother, Elaine, was equally remarkable. As the principal of Benson High School, Elaine had built a reputation as one of the best in the district. Her school boasted an A rating, and she was beloved by students and parents alike. At five feet tall, Elaine's presence was as commanding as her stylish wardrobe. Her long, naturally curly hair framed her face with effortless grace. Known for attending every school event and game, Elaine fostered an unbreakable sense of community.

Marie loved going to football games with her mother. It wasn't just the thrill of the game that excited her; it was the chance to see Marcellus.

Marcellus was everything Marie dreamed of in a boy. He was an all-around athlete at Benson High School, and he excelled on the field and in the classroom, consistently ranking at the top of his class. At 6 feet 3 inches tall, with long braids, a dark brown complexion, and hazel eyes, Marcellus' bright, confident smile could make anyone's day. His dreams of becoming an NFL player and, later, a commentator reflected his ambition and drive. And though Marcellus was focused on his goals, he couldn't help but notice Marie.

ΛΛΛΛΛΛΛΛΛΛΛΛΛΛΛΛΛΛΛΛΛΛΛΛΛΛΛΛ

One Friday evening, Marie and her mother attended a Benson High game. As usual, Marie and Marcellus met near the bathrooms on the opposing team's side. But this time, there was something different in the air. Marcellus took a deep breath, his heart pounding in his chest. Finally, he mustered the courage.

"Marie," he began nervously, "I've been meaning to ask you something for a while."

Marie tilted her head, curious. "What is it, Marcellus?"

Marcellus hesitated for a moment, then blurted out, "Will you be my girlfriend?"

Marie's eyes widened in surprise. A grin spread across her face as she nodded quickly. "Yes! Of course, I will!"

Relieved and overjoyed, Marcellus leaned in and kissed Marie's cheek. They walked hand in hand back to where Principal Elaine was sitting, cheering on the game.

"Wait," Marie said suddenly, her steps faltering. "Marcellus, what are you doing?"

"I'm going to tell your mom about us," Marcellus said confidently.

"Are you crazy? She doesn't even like me talking to boys!" Marie hissed, her voice barely a whisper.

Marcellus squeezed her hand reassuringly. "Don't worry. I'll handle it."

When they reached Principal Elaine, Marcellus cleared his throat and spoke up. "Principal Elaine, I need to talk to you."

Principal Elaine turned her attention to the pair, her eyebrow arching in curiosity. "What's on your mind, Marcellus?"

Marcellus shifted nervously but held his ground. "Well…I asked Marie to be my girlfriend, and she said yes."

Marie stared at the ground, avoiding her mother's piercing gaze. She cleared her throat and fidgeted with her hands as her mother processed the news.

"Excuse me?" Principal Elaine said, crossing her arms. "You two just met right, and now you're in a relationship? How long has this been going on?"

Marcellus answered honestly, "We met at the first football game of the year."

Principal Elaine's eyes narrowed. "And why am I just now hearing about this?"

Marie finally spoke up, her voice barely audible. "I didn't tell you because I know how you feel about me liking boys before I graduate from college."

Principal Elaine shook her head, a small smile tugging at her lips. "Marie, I'm not saying you can't have friends who are boys. But jumping straight into a relationship? You both need to take it slow."

Marcellus nodded earnestly. "We understand, Principal Elaine. We promise to be responsible."

Principal Elaine sighed, her expression softening. "All right. You can be friends."

Marcellus grinned mischievously. "Boyfriend-girlfriend friends?"

Principal Elaine rolled her eyes but chuckled. "Fine. But remember, I'm watching you two."

Chapter Two

The Girls

Marie couldn't wait to tell her friends the news. During lunch the next day, she gathered her closest friends, Catherine, Tasha, and Brielle, at their usual spot near the window in the cafeteria.

"So," Marie began, unable to hide her grin, "I have some big news."

Catherine immediately perked up. "Ooh, spill it!"

Marie leaned in, her voice barely above a whisper. "Marcellus asked me to be his girlfriend last night."

The table erupted into squeals and laughter. "Girl, are you serious?" Tasha asked, her eyes wide with excitement.

"Yes! And my mom knows about him now, too."

Catherine smirked, leaning back in her chair. "Well, well, Marie. Now you can finally be like us."

Marie frowned. "What does that mean?"

Catherine rolled her eyes playfully. "It just means you're part of the club now. You have a boyfriend, just like we do."

"I just got a boyfriend and I'm still processing it," Marie said.

"True," Catherine said, shrugging. "But still, you're one of us. Except my boyfriend walks me to class and kisses me all day."

Marie scrunched up her nose. "Yuck. I don't want to kiss all day."

"You will," Catherine said knowingly. "The more you like him, the more you'll want to kiss him."

Marie shook her head firmly. "No, I won't. Kissing is just the precursor to sex. I am not interested in any of that."

Catherine raised an eyebrow. "Girl, let me tell you something. If you don't give it up to Marcellus, someone else will."

Marie's jaw tightened. "And someone else will have to, Catherine. That's not happening with me."

The table fell silent for a moment before Brielle chimed in. "She's serious, Catherine. Marie's not like that, and we all know Marcellus likes her for who she is."

"Okay, okay," Catherine said, throwing up her hands. "I'm just saying. Boys have needs, and you need to be prepared for that."

Marie's stomach churned, but she held her ground. "I don't need to prepare for anything except graduating high school next year. Period."

Chapter Three

A Mother's Wisdom

That night, Elaine called Marie into the kitchen for one of her trademark talks, the kind that felt part lesson, part sermon, and always hit the mark. Marie sat at the table, nervously twisting a strand of her hair, wondering what direction her mom was about to take.

"Marie," Elaine began, her tone calm yet commanding, "I know Marcellus is a good boy. He's smart, respectful, and well-mannered. But don't let all that blind you. At the end of the day, he's still a boy. And you know what boys are often thinking about."

Marie groaned softly. "Mom, I know. You don't have to spell it out."

"Oh, I'm going to spell it out," Elaine countered, her left eyebrow arching. "Because it's important you understand that a lot of boys don't know what they really want, not even Marcellus. And if you're not careful, you'll find yourself tangled up in something you never planned for."

"I get it, Mom," Marie said, her tone defensive.

"Do you?" Elaine leaned forward, her voice dropping into her signature boss-queen mode. "Listen to me, Marie. Don't get caught up chasing 'feelings' or trying to label what you have. Forget the whole idea of love. For now, just take it out of the equation. You keep it cool. You keep it, friendship. You stay level-headed, and guess what? You'll be good for life."

Marie looked confused. "What do you mean, 'good for life'?"

"I mean this: when you don't let emotions cloud your judgment, you make smart decisions. You see people for who they are, not who you want them to be. And when things don't go your way, you can walk away without the weight of regret dragging you down. That's how you stay strong, Marie. That's how you win."

Marie sat back, taking in her mother's words.

Elaine continued, her voice firm yet loving. "You need to think of boys like Marcellus as practice for life, not the main event. Learn how to read people, how to set boundaries, and how to keep your dignity intact no matter what happens. Feelings are nice, but they don't pay the price when things fall apart. You do. So don't give anyone that power over you."

Marie nodded slowly. "So, you're saying…keep it light and keep it moving?"

Elaine smiled faintly, a gleam of pride in her eyes. "Exactly, Baby Girl. If it's meant to grow into something real, it will. But until then, don't let anyone take you off your game."

Marie looked down at the table, absorbing every word. "I hear you, Mom. I'll be careful."

"I know you will," Elaine said, squeezing her daughter's hand. "Because you're my daughter, and I raised you to know your worth. Just remember, no boy, no matter how sweet he seems, deserves your tears or your peace of mind. Keep it classy, keep it cool, and you'll be just fine. Oh, and call your dad and tell him soon. Don't let him hear about you and your so-called boyfriend from anyone else."

Marie smiled softly, feeling both reassured and empowered. She didn't fully understand how her mom had managed to blend wisdom and street smarts into such a seamless package, but she knew one thing for sure: her mother was a queen, and she was determined to live up to that legacy. "I will call my dad tomorrow, Mom. I definitely want to be the one to tell him."

Chapter Four

A Warning From Charlotte

Later that evening, Marie called her cousin Charlotte, who was more like a big sister to her. Charlotte answered on the second ring, and you could feel her excitement.

"Marie! I heard you've got yourself a boyfriend now!"

Marie giggled. "Who told you?"

"Your mom called me this morning. Who do you think told me?" Charlotte said. "She said Marcellus is a good kid, but you know how she is."

Marie sighed. "Yeah, she had the talk with me last night. Anyway, I wanted to tell you myself. I'm so happy, Charlotte."

"I'm happy for you too, but… how are you going to make this work?"

Marie frowned. "What do you mean?"

"You're always busy with school activities and work. You'll barely see him except maybe on weekends. How are you going to keep that connection alive?"

"We'll go out on weekends and talk on the phone every day," Marie said confidently.

Charlotte chuckled. "And what about all the little fast girls at school?"

Marie's voice grew firm. "He's with me. He doesn't want anyone else. Plus, I am at the school; they know better."

"They don't care, Marie. And listen, I'm telling you as someone who's been there, don't start giving up your virginity just because you think it'll keep him. That was my biggest mistake."

"I'm not," Marie said quickly.

"I'm serious," Charlotte continued. "Boys know how to say all the right things. They'll lie to you, make promises, and then the next thing you know, you're dealing with heartbreak, or worse, a pregnancy, or an STD."

Marie shuddered. "Charlotte, you're making it sound so scary."

"Good," Charlotte said bluntly. "A little fear will keep you safe. Boys don't want us. They want what we can give them."

"Marcellus isn't like that," Marie said softly.

"Just watch out, okay?" Charlotte replied.

"I will. Thanks, Charlotte."

Chapter Five

The Boys

Marcellus couldn't stop talking about Marie to his friends. After basketball practice, he and his closest boys, Dakar, Michael, and Jace, lingered in the locker room, tossing around jokes and basketballs, their conversation inevitably turning to Marcellus' promising relationship.

"Man, I still can't believe you pulled Marie," Dakar said, shaking his head as he tied his sneakers.

Marcellus grinned, leaning back against a locker. "Why not? You know I've got game."

"Nah, it's not just game," Michael said, throwing a basketball into the air. "Marie's not like these other girls. She's different; classy. Always smiling, always looking like she's ready to walk into a boardroom or something."

"And she's got brains," Dakar added, slapping Marcellus on the back. "Straight A's, student council president, volunteering; she's the whole package, bro. A certified wifey."

Marcellus nodded, his grin fading into a serious expression. "That's why I'm not rushing anything. I don't want to mess this up."

"You're smart," Jace said, leaning against the wall. "Girls like Marie don't come around often. But don't sleep on the fact that her dad is a whole different story."

"What do you mean?" Marcellus asked, narrowing his eyes.

Dakar smirked. "Bro, everyone knows about Mr. Tucker. That man doesn't play. He's like a human lie detector."

"And don't forget Principal Elaine," Michael said, laughing. "Marie's mom is the real deal. She's tough but fair. If you mess up, she'll know before you even realize what you did."

"Y'all are acting like I'm walking into a job interview or something," Marcellus said, rolling his eyes.

"That's because you are," Jace said, tossing the basketball back to Michael. "You don't just date a girl like Marie. You date her whole family."

"Speaking of her family," Michael added with a smirk, "don't sleep on Principal Elaine. She's a knockout. If Marie's anything like her mom, you've hit the jackpot."

Marcellus shook his head, laughing. "Man, don't start crushing on her mom now."

The boys erupted into laughter, their voices echoing through the locker room.

But behind the jokes, Marcellus felt the weight of their words. Meeting Marie's dad wasn't going to be a walk in the park, but if he wanted to be with Marie, he knew he would have to step up to the plate.

Chapter Six

A Father's Love

Marie contemplated calling her dad, but then decided now would be the perfect time. DeWayne Tucker was the definition of OG. One of Omaha, Nebraska's original gangsters, he was a man who commanded respect the moment he walked into a room. Standing at 5'11", with caramel-brown skin that seemed to glow under the sun, DeWayne had a tight, flawless fade and a crisp, sexy goatee that stayed sharp no matter the day. His body? A masterpiece. He was a workout buff with sculpted pecs and arms that could intimidate or embrace, you'd be lucky to experience either.

But DeWayne wasn't just a powerhouse in looks. He had the charm to match. A smooth talker with a golden tongue, he could talk his way out of a corner or into a woman's heart without breaking a sweat. Women adored him, and he knew it, but he carried himself with a cool confidence that made him untouchable.

DeWayne and Elaine were the ultimate duo when they got married young. They were unstoppable, passionate, and full of fire. But after 13 years, life had its way of pulling them in different directions. They grew apart, but the love they shared never faded. Even after their divorce, they stayed best friends, proving that sometimes love doesn't end, it just changes. They were better apart but always there for each other, showing the world what true respect and connection look like. DeWayne wasn't just a man. He was a legacy, a force, and a father who left a mark wherever he went.

§§§§§§§§§§§§§§§§§§§§§§§§§§§§§§

The phone rang, cutting through the quiet of the evening. Marie clutched the receiver tightly, nerves creeping up her spine. On the other end, her father, DeWayne, answered in his usual deep, commanding tone.

"Hello?"

"Hi, Dad! How are you?" Marie's voice came out brighter than she intended, an effort to mask her unease.

"Hey there, Princess. I'm good. And you?"
"I'm good too, Dad. I, uh…I actually have something I need to tell you."

DeWayne let out a low chuckle, the kind that hinted he already knew this was about to be serious. "Oh boy. What's going on, Princess? Spit it out."

Marie hesitated, twisting the hem of her shirt in her fingers. Finally, she took a deep breath. "I...I have a boyfriend, Dad."

The line went silent momentarily, and then DeWayne's voice returned, sharp but measured. "A boyfriend? Really? And how long has this been going on?"

"A few months. We've been friends for a while, and it kind of just happened. He just asked me yesterday."

"And what's this boy's name?"

"His name is Marcellus, Dad. Marcellus Hall."

The name seemed to hit DeWayne like a bolt. There was a beat of silence before he barked a laugh. "Marcellus Hall? Wait a minute, Jerome Hall's boy? Are we talking about the same Marcellus?"

Marie's stomach flipped. "You know his dad?"

"Of course I do. Jerome and I go way back to when we were running the streets together. Good people, the Halls. But still, Princess, a boyfriend? Why the rush?"

Marie groaned lightly, rolling her eyes even though he couldn't see. "Dad, it's not a rush. I like him. He's sweet, respectful, and he treats me well."

DeWayne's voice softened for a moment. "That's good. But let me give you some advice, Princess. Love is nice, but don't get too caught up in your feelings. Keep your head in the game."

Marie frowned. "What do you mean?"

"I mean," DeWayne said, his tone turning slightly more serious, "you've gotta stay cool. Don't let your emotions run wild. When you're all caught up in feelings, it's hard to see straight. Keep it simple. Be cool. That way, if something goes left, you can walk away without looking back."

Marie fell silent, unsure how to respond.

DeWayne continued; his voice now tinged with a bit of his old-school swagger. "Listen, love is good, but it ain't worth losing your sense. A real man will respect you for staying grounded, and if he doesn't, well, then he's not your man. Understand?"

"Yes, Dad," Marie said quietly.

"Good," DeWayne said firmly. "And one more thing, this Marcellus boy needs to meet me. Any guy serious about my daughter has to go through me first. That's the rule."

Marie sighed. "Okay, Dad. I'll tell him."

"Good. Remember, you're my baby girl. No boy, not even Jerome Hall's son, is gonna play games with you."

"I know, Dad. I love you."

"I love you too, Princess. Now keep your head up and stay sharp. You hear me?"

Marie smiled softly, feeling a mix of embarrassment and gratitude. "I hear you, Dad. Bye."

"Bye, Princess."

As Marie hung up, she let out a deep breath. She knew her father's advice came from a place of love, but it was still a lot to take in. Looking at the phone, Marie muttered to herself, "This just got way more complicated."

Chapter Seven

The Question

Marie's phone rang, and her face lit up when she saw Marcellus's name on the screen. She picked up on the second ring.

"Hey there, Marie," Marcellus said with his smooth, confident tone.

"Hey, Marcellus," Marie replied, a soft smile spreading across her face.

"What are you doing this weekend?" Marcellus asked casually.

"Nothing much. Why?"

"Well, I was thinking about heading to the mall and catching a movie. I'd love for you to join me."

Marie felt a flutter of excitement. "That sounds like so much fun! Thank you for asking me."

"Cool! There's a boxing movie I've been wanting to see. It starts at 2:00 PM. You like boxing?"

"I love boxing," Marie said eagerly. "And 2:00 PM sounds perfect."

Marcellus paused. "Actually, I was thinking maybe we could meet earlier, say around noon? That way, we'd have some extra time to hang out before the movie."

Marie hesitated. "That sounds great, but I don't think I can ride with you."

Marcellus chuckled. "Oh, I figured that much. Your mom and dad are pretty strict, huh?"

"You have no idea," Marie replied, laughing. "They'll probably insist on driving me there and picking me up."

"That's cool. I respect that," Marcellus said with a smile in his voice. "I just look forward to spending time with you, no matter how you get there."

Marie blushed. "Me too."

"Alright then, it's a date. I'll see you Saturday."

"See you then."

"Bye, Marie."

"Goodbye, Marcellus."

Marie hung up, grinning ear to ear. But her excitement was quickly replaced with nervousness. "What am I going to wear? And what if Dad insists on embarrassing me in front of Marcellus?" She groaned. "Why does this have to be so complicated?

Chapter Eight
Meet the Parents

Marie blushed and frowned and contemplated with herself. Her thoughts were tempered by the reality of her family dynamics. As much as she liked Marcellus, she knew this wasn't going to be a simple date. She called him back.

"Hey, Marcellus," Marie said, her tone more serious.

"Marie! What's up?" Marcellus's voice was light, but he could sense a shift.

"Listen, before we can go on this date, there's something we need to handle first," Marie began.

Marcellus laughed softly. "What, you have to get permission from your parents or something?"

"N…n…not just permission," Marie said. "You have to meet my dad."

There was silence on the line for a moment. "Your dad?" Marcellus repeated, his tone more cautious now.

"Yes," Marie confirmed. "And just so you know, he already knows who you are."

"Wait… what?"

"Your dad, Jerome Hall? My dad knows him. They go way back. So, yeah, you've got to come by the house first. I will let my dad know when."

Marcellus let out a low whistle. "Oh man, this just got real."

Marie smiled despite her nerves. "It's not as bad as it sounds. My mom will be there too, and she knows you're a good guy. But my dad, well, he's protective. He'll want to know your intentions and all that."

Marcellus cleared his throat. "Alright. When does this meeting of the minds happen?"

"Let's do Friday night," Marie responded. "Be here at 7:00 PM sharp. And Marcellus?"

"Yeah?"

"Be yourself. My dad might act tough, but he respects honesty. Just tell him who you are and what you're about."

"You got it," Marcellus said, his confidence returning. "I'll see you Friday."

Chapter Nine

Friday

The doorbell rang at exactly 7:00 PM Marie's heart raced as she opened the door to find Marcellus standing there, dressed in a crisp button-down shirt and jeans, holding a bouquet of flowers.

"These are for Principal Elaine, I mean your mom," Marcellus said, handing the bouquet over with a shy smile.

Elaine appeared behind Marie, her face lighting up at the gesture. "Why, thank you, Marcellus. These are lovely. Come on in."

As Marcellus stepped inside, his eyes immediately landed on DeWayne, seated at the head of the dining table, his presence commanding the room.

"So, you're Jerome's boy," DeWayne said, his deep voice filling the space.

"Yes, Sir," Marcellus replied, standing tall.

DeWayne gestured to the chair across from him. "Have a seat."

Marie sat next to her mother, her eyes darting nervously between her father and Marcellus.

"So, Marcellus," DeWayne began, his gaze steady. "What are your dreams? Your goals? What do you see for your future?"

Marcellus didn't hesitate. "I'm on the honor roll at school, Sir. Straight A's. I plan to go to college, maybe study engineering. I want to build something, you know? Something that lasts. I believe after I graduate from college, I will go to the NFL, and I would also like to later on be an NFL commentator, but if not, I will be an engineer, so I will be good."

DeWayne leaned back, studying Marcellus. "That's a good answer. But why Marie? What's your reasoning for liking my daughter?"

Marcellus glanced at Marie, then back at DeWayne. "Because she's different. She's smart, kind, and she doesn't play games. She's real, and I respect that."

Elaine smiled, chiming in. "I've seen Marcellus around school. He's a good student and respectful to his teachers. He's not like most boys his age."

DeWayne nodded slowly, but his tone remained firm. "Respect is good, but it's not enough. If you want to spend time with my daughter, you need to

35

understand one thing: this isn't a game. You treat her right, or you'll answer to me. Got it?"

"Yes, Sir," Marcellus said earnestly.

Elaine leaned forward. "And Marcellus, what's your plan for this relationship? Because we don't do flings in this family. We value commitment and integrity."

Marcellus swallowed but held his ground. "I don't have all the answers, Principal Elaine, but I know I like Marie. And I'm willing to prove that to both of you."

Marie's heart swelled with pride as she watched Marcellus stand his ground.

DeWayne finally broke into a rare smile. "Alright, Son. You've got my permission to take Marie out. But remember, no funny business. And she's home by 9:00 PM."

Marcellus stood, extending his hand. "Thank you, Sir. I won't let you down."

As they left the table, Elaine caught Marie's eye and winked. "He's a good one, Sweetheart. But keep your head on straight."

Marie nodded, her heart full as she walked Marcellus to the door. "You did great," she whispered.

"Thanks," Marcellus replied, his grin widening. "Now, about that movie tomorrow..."

Marie laughed, feeling a sense of excitement and relief. This was just the beginning.

Chapter Ten

The Date

Man, let me tell you about the wildest day ever—me and Marcellus shut it all the way down! From the moment he rolled up to my house to the second I walked back through that door at 8:15 sharp, it was nothing but laughs, good vibes, and memories to last forever. First off, my dad had to do his whole "tough guy" act before letting me ride with Marcellus to the mall and movies. You know the deal, firm handshake, piercing stare, and that "you better respect my daughter or else" energy. Marcellus passed the test, again of course. My dad even said, "That boy's got too much respect for me and your mom to try anything." Like, okay, Dad. Cool story.

But I'll admit, it worked. Marcellus was on his absolute best behavior, which lowkey made me feel some type of way. I didn't want him trying anything, but dang, I wanted it to be known that Marcellus respected me because he cared about me, not because he was scared of my dad! Still, I can't front, Marcellus made the day perfect.

We hit the photo booths at the mall, snapping pictures like two fools, duck faces, goofy smiles, and straight-up clowning around until we were falling out laughing. People probably thought we were crazy, but we didn't care. Then we hit the theater for this boxing movie that was absolutely fire! I mean, every punch and knockout had us hyped, whispering our predictions and cracking up at each other's reactions.

And the snacks? Legendary. Popcorn, Twizzlers, and root beer, the ultimate combo. Turns out, we both love all three. We kept stealing from each other's stash, even though we had plenty, because why not? By the end of the movie, we were laughing more at ourselves than anything else.

By the time I got home, I was still smiling about something Marcellus said. For real, I have my girls, and they're amazing, but there's something different about hanging out with a guy like Marcellus. He's honest, cool, and easy to talk to. No arguments, no drama, no side-eye moments. Just pure amazing energy. I could do this again and again. Best. Day. Ever.

Chapter Eleven
Ring Ring

"Ring, ring."

"What's up?" Marcellus answered, his tone calm, though he already knew the voice on the other end wasn't bringing peace.

"Yeah, what's up, Marcellus?" P'Trice shouted, her voice sharp and cutting.

Marcellus sighed, pinching the bridge of his nose. "What do you need, and why are you yelling, P'Trice?"

"Oh, don't play dumb with me," P'Trice snapped. "So, you got a new girlfriend, huh? Some hood rat named Marie? That's what's up now?"

Marcellus' grip on the phone tightened. "First of all, Marie is far from that. She's classy, intelligent, and driven, everything you're not. Watch your mouth when you talk about her."

P'Trice let out a bitter laugh. "Classy? Please. She's just another basic girl trying to act like she belongs. Word on the street is she's all smiles and no substance. She's not even on my level."

"You didn't hear that anywhere," Marcellus shot back, his voice cold. "You're just bitter and making stuff up. Whatever game you're trying to play, I'm not in it."

"Oh, I'm bitter?" P'Trice said, her tone dripping with sarcasm. "You're the one walking around the mall and the movies all boo'd up like some love-struck fool. You're embarrassing yourself with this girl."

Marcellus shook his head. "What's embarrassing is this conversation. You don't see me blowing up your phone, so why are you blowing up mine?"

"You're mine, Marcellus!" P'Trice's voice cracked with emotion. "We were supposed to be forever. How can you just forget that?"

"Forever ended when you started running around with Alonzo and Tate," Marcellus said firmly. "Don't act like you didn't make your choice. You're not hurt because I moved on; you're mad because you thought I'd wait for you."

P'Trice's voice softened, the venom replaced with desperation. "They didn't mean anything, Marcellus. It's always been you. You know that."

Marcellus rolled his eyes. "It's never been me, P'Trice. Let's keep it real. You loved the idea of me, but you didn't know how to appreciate what you had. Now it's too late."

"Too late?" P'Trice said, her voice rising again. "We'll see about that. I'm on my way over."

Before Marcellus could respond, the line went dead.

Chapter Twelve

P'Trice

As she rummaged through her closet, P'Trice muttered under her breath, her anger simmering. "Tate and Alonzo were such a joke. Neither of them cared about me the way Marcellus did. And now he's running around with some nobody? He's out of his mind." P'Trice yanked a sleek black dress off its hanger, holding it up against herself in the mirror.

Her reflection stared back, determined and fiery. "Marcellus was the best thing that ever happened to me, and I let him slip away. Not anymore. If I have to remind him what we had, and show that little Marie who she's dealing with, then so be it."

Slipping into the dress, P'Trice smoothed it over her hips and applied a bold red lipstick. "Marie doesn't stand a chance," she said with a smirk. "I'm not letting him go without a fight."

Marcellus had just settled on the couch, flipping through his notes for tomorrow's big test, when he heard a sharp knock at the door. He sighed deeply, already knowing who it was.

When he opened the door, there stood P'Trice, dressed to kill, her smirk as confident as ever.

"What are you doing here, P'Trice?"

"You know why I'm here," P'Trice said, brushing past Marcellus into the house without waiting for an invitation.

Marcellus closed the door, crossing his arms. "We don't have anything to talk about."

"Funny," P'Trice said, leaning casually against the wall. "Because I think your little girlfriend would love to hear about us. You didn't tell her about me, did you?"

Marcellus raised an eyebrow. "There's nothing to tell. You're my ex, P'Trice. You don't matter."

"Don't matter?" P'Trice's voice turned venomous. "You think she'll still be smiling when she sees the pictures I have? Or when she hears how you used to call me late at night?"

Marcellus clenched his jaw, his voice low. "You're pathetic. Do you think dragging up old memories is going to change anything? Marie isn't stupid! She'll see right through you."

"Oh, I'm the pathetic one?" P'Trice sneered, stepping closer. "We'll see who's pathetic when Marie dumps you for being the liar you are."

Marcellus laughed bitterly. "This isn't about me or Marie. This is about you being miserable and trying to drag everyone down with you. But I'm not falling for it, and neither is Marie."

P'Trice's smirk faltered for a moment before she regained her composure. "We'll see about that." With one last glare, she turned on her heel and walked out, slamming the door behind her.

Marcellus stood there for a moment, running a hand through his hair. He knew P'Trice wasn't done, and he hated the thought of Marie being dragged into the mess.

"Drama always finds a way," Marcellus muttered to himself, his mind already racing with how to handle the storm P'Trice was about to unleash.

Chapter Thirteen
Messy Moves

Marie sat at the kitchen table, flipping through her algebra textbook when the phone rang. Something made her glance at the screen. The caller ID read Unknown. Against her better judgment, she answered.

"Hello?" Marie said cautiously.

"Well, hello there," a smug, sharp voice replied. "You don't know me, but you should. Let's just say we have something, or someone in common."

Marie's brow furrowed. "Who is this?"

The voice on the other end practically dripped with arrogance. "Oh, Sweetie it's P'Trice. You know, Marcellus's real girl."

Marie's heart skipped a beat, but she quickly steadied herself. "What do you want?"

P'Trice chuckled darkly. "Just thought you'd want to know your little boyfriend isn't as loyal as he seems. Word around town is he was all up in the mall and at the movies last weekend. And guess who was with him? Me."

Marie's jaw tightened, but she kept her composure. "Funny, because I was at the mall and the movies with Marcellus. So, unless you were there with us, this sounds like a desperate lie."

P'Trice snapped, her tone turning venomous. "I just wanted to see if you're the one they are talking about, but I was with him last weekend. Let me tell you something, you're temporary. I've been in Marcellus's life longer than you, and I'll still be around when you're long gone."

Marie smirked, though her voice remained calm. "You sound pressed, P'Trice. You can try to intimidate me, but let me make one thing clear: I'm not scared of you. And if you thought calling me was going to make me back down, you've got the wrong one."

The silence on the other end spoke volumes. Before P'Trice could respond, Marie hung up, shaking her head.

Chapter Fourteen

The Next Day

The next day at school, the rumor mill was in full swing. By lunchtime, whispers of "Did you hear about Marcellus and P'Trice?" filled the air. Marie walked into the cafeteria, feeling the weight of every stare. She sat down at her usual table, where her best friend Tasha was waiting.

"Tasha, what is going on?" Marie asked.

Tasha sighed. "P'Trice has been running her mouth all morning. She's telling people she and Marcellus hooked up last weekend. She even said she's got proof."

Marie's stomach churned. "What proof?"

Tasha shrugged. "She's got a picture. She's showing it around like a trophy."

§§§§§§§§§§§§§§§§§§§§§§§§§§§§§§

Marie caught up with Marcellus after his football practice. She stood by the locker room door, arms crossed, waiting for him to come out. When he saw her, his face lit up, until he noticed her expression.

"Marie, what's wrong?"

"You tell me," Marie snapped. "Why is P'Trice telling everyone she was with you last weekend?"

Marcellus frowned. "She's lying. I haven't seen P'Trice since…" He paused, running a hand over his face. "Since forever. She's trying to mess with your head."

Marie shook her head. "She has a picture, Marcellus. And people are starting to believe her."

Marcellus grabbed Marie's hands. "Marie, listen to me. I don't care what she says or what picture she's flashing around. I haven't done anything. You have to trust me."

Marie pulled away. "Trust is earned, Marcellus. And right now, I don't know what to believe." Marie turned and walked away, leaving Marcellus standing there.

§§§§§§§§§§§§§§§§§§§§§§§§§§§§§§§§

Later that afternoon, Marie decided she had had enough. She found P'Trice near the school parking lot, surrounded by a group of students.

"P'Trice!" Marie called, her voice cutting through the chatter.

P'Trice turned, smirking when she saw Marie. "Well, if it isn't the lady of the hour. What can I do for you, sweetheart?"

Marie stepped forward. "Cut the crap. Why are you lying about Marcellus?"

P'Trice tilted her head, looking innocent. "Lying? Oh, Honey, I don't lie. I just tell the truth people don't want to hear."

"Show me the picture," Marie demanded.

P'Trice pulled a Polaroid from her bag and held it up for everyone to see. The photo showed her and Marcellus sitting on a couch, laughing.

"See?" P'Trice said smugly. "Proof."

Marie snatched the photo and examined it closely. Her eyes narrowed. "This isn't from last weekend. Look at the date on the calendar in the background. It's from last year." The crowd murmured as they noticed the detail.

P'Trice's smirk faltered. "Doesn't matter. The point is, he was with me first. And he'll come back to me."

Marie stepped closer, her voice steady. "You can keep living in the past, P'Trice. But Marcellus has moved on. Maybe you should, too." The crowd erupted in cheers and laughter as P'Trice stormed off, her plan backfiring spectacularly.

Chapter Fifteen

Marcellus Apology

That evening, Marcellus showed up at Marie's house, holding a bouquet of flowers.

"Marie, I'm sorry you had to deal with all this," he said. "I should've warned you about P'Trice. She's been holding onto something that ended a long time ago."

Marie took the flowers but didn't invite Marcellus in. "You need to make sure P'Trice gets the message, Marcellus. Because I won't be dragged into her mess again."

"I will," Marcellus promised. "I'll make it clear there's no going back."

Marie nodded, but her trust in Marcellus was shaken.

Chapter Sixteen

Recap

Before I dive into everything else, let me do a recap and take you back to where it all began with Marcellus. Good guy? Definitely. Great guy? Absolutely. He was fun, magnetic, the kind of young man everyone wanted to be around. But let me tell you, his world came with baggage.

See, Marcellus had this thing for these girls that I had no idea about. They loved his popularity, his status, and the way he carried himself. And trust me, he loved the attention. Patrice? Oh, she was just the first one in a long line of drama. Marcellus knew how to run these girls, no doubt about it. He had them wrapped around his finger, doing whatever he wanted.

But here's the thing, Marcellus never ran me. From day one, he treated me differently. He didn't treat me like some side piece or fling. He treated me like a queen. No games, no disrespect, no nonsense. And because of that, I respected him. I wasn't like those other girls. I didn't fall for the hype or the lifestyle. I didn't love Marcellus for what he had or who wanted him, I loved him. I loved his soul. I loved the guy he was beneath all the attention, the popularity, and the chaos.

What we had was deeper. Our connection wasn't built on surface stuff. It was friendship, trust, and a bond that no one could shake. Marcellus and I never broke up because there was nothing to break. We didn't end; we just adjusted. Life pulled us in different directions, but we always found our way back to each other. That's what happens when something is real, it doesn't fade.

I've always been that chick for Marcellus. Always. And I've always known that no one could take my place. Girls have come and gone, but me? I've been solid from day one, and he's always known it. That's why we are where we are today.

Marie and Marcellus, that's where it started. But buckle up, because where we're headed next? That's a whole other crazy story. Stay tuned.

Chapter Seventeen 1995

Fast Forward

His and Hers Salon was the crown jewel of Ames Street. High-class, polished, and professionally run, it was the spot where style met sophistication. The moment you walked in, you were greeted by the warm, inviting scent of high-end products and fresh flowers, a signature blend that instantly made you feel like royalty.

Barbers lined one side, masters of their craft, creating fades and cuts so clean they could stop traffic. On the other side, hairdressers worked their magic, transforming ordinary hair into extraordinary works of art. Every chair in the salon was a throne, and every client left looking like a million bucks.

But let's be real. This wasn't just a salon. His and Hers was also the spot for tea-spilling, shade-throwing, and all-out gossip. There was always someone, somewhere, running their mouth about something, or someone, and the talkers were completely oblivious to who might be listening. And today was no exception.

The buzzing crowd, the packed parking lot, and the unmistakable energy in the air hinted that something big was brewing. As usual, the owner Mrs. B.

was outside, directing traffic with her no-nonsense attitude, but inside? Inside, words were flying fast and loose. Tongues wagged about someone's man, someone's business, and someone's secrets. Little did they know, one of those someone's was about to be Marie.

And Marie? Well, Marie didn't take kindly to being the topic of conversation. The second she caught wind of the whispers, it was game over. Tonight was about to take a sharp left turn, and someone was about to learn why Marie was not the one to play with.

Marie leaned against the counter at the packed salon, looking for a snack to buy, while Catherine flipped through a magazine. Marie wasn't paying attention until a girl named Asia's voice rose above the buzz.

"Girl, I miss my James Loco," Asia said with a playful laugh. "I'm tired of Dolla and his mess. I should've stayed with James anyway. He's loyal, got that car looking good now, and knows how to treat me. Me and him are going to sneak off and kick it this weekend."

Marie's ears burned. "James Loco? Loyal? Treats her right?" A pit of rage began forming in her stomach. She tried to play it cool, but her nails dug into her palm.

"Hold up," Kim, the stylist, said, chuckling with Asia. "How you getting away with this Asia?"

Asia smirked. "I just gotta start a little argument with Dolla. He'll storm out, and boom, I'm free."

Marie's jaw tightened. Catherine nudged her. "You hearing this?" Catherine whispered, her eyes wide.

Marie's lips curved into a slow, dangerous smile. "Oh, I'm hearing it. But she's not the only one who can play dirty."

"What are you trying to do?" Catherine asked, because Catherine knew Marie was about that business when it came to shutting foolishness down.

"Trying? No Baby, I am going to meet Dolla tonight! I am not the one to play with. I'll take your man."

"Here we go," Catherine stated.

"Right, because we've got to finish what Asia and James Loco started. Tonight is going to be a good night," Marie said laughing. Marie slid into Kim's chair with the confidence of a queen taking her throne. Kim, the best in the game, didn't just do hair, she created masterpieces, and tonight was no different. As the flat iron glided through Marie's strands, the room seemed to pause, mesmerized by the transformation.

When Kim finished, Marie's hair was a showstopper, sleek, shiny, and flawless. Whenever she turned her head, her hair flew like silk caught in a perfect breeze, shimmering under the salon lights. It was the kind of look that turned heads, stopped conversations, and demanded attention.

Marie wasn't just ready to take on the night, she owned the night before it even started. With every strand in place and her confidence on full display, she was a force. And anyone daring enough to cross her path tonight? Well, they wouldn't forget her name.

Chapter Eighteen
Betrayal Unveiled

I just want to explain what happened so you will fully understand why I was so upset with Asia and James Loco. I am not one for public scenes or messy confrontations. I keep my business tight, my circle small, and my heart guarded. But when Asia's careless chatter filled the air of the crowded salon, everything changed. Even though she didn't know who I was or what me and James Loco had going on, she was reckless.

Let me tell you, Asia was sitting there, loud as ever, running her mouth about her plans for the night. And guess what? Those plans involved my James. The nerve of it. The sheer audacity. My blood ran cold hearing her. James isn't just some man; he's my man.

Now, our relationship? It was not your typical storybook romance. It was lowkey, exclusive, and built on honesty and respect. That's how we liked it. No one really knew I was James girl, just me and Catherine and James and a few of his friends.

James, he's got this nerdy gangster thing going on. He was a college graduate turned streetwise, with dark brown skin, gold chains, and those black glasses that made him look like a professor and a hustler all at once.

Even though we kept our business private it was still a slap in the face for Asia to be out here, in public, claiming she's got something going on with James. She has no idea who's man that is! And James? He was supposed to be better than this. We had a deal, no outsiders, and no secrets. If anything changed, we'd talk it out.

But instead, Asia's sitting there, bragging like she owns the place, making a joke of everything James and I built. And James? If he's stepping out, he owes me a conversation, not this public betrayal.

My mind was racing, replaying every moment with James, searching for signs I might've missed. But there was nothing. James was perfect, I thought.

I'm not one to beg for loyalty or hand out second chances. James crossed a line, and he was about to see exactly who he was dealing with. I don't do drama, but I don't back down either. This isn't about revenge. It's about reminding myself, of my worth. I play smart. And when I'm done, everyone knows I'm a force to be reckoned with.

I walked out of that salon with my head held high, ready for what was about to come next, me meeting Dolla. Actions speak louder than words, and trust me, this was just the beginning.

Chapter Nineteen

Dolla

That evening, Marie put her plan into motion. After some digging and a few discreet calls, she had Dolla's hangout location, his style, and even knew the kind of drinks he liked. If Asia wanted her James, Marie was about to make a move on Dolla.

As they cruised through the city, Catherine kept asking, "You sure about this? What if he's bad news?"

"Bad news?" Marie laughed, her voice dripping with sass. "Girl, I am the bad news."

Catherine laughed out loud. "Girl, you wild. Let's see if Dolla can handle all that energy."

§§§§§§§§§§§§§§§§§§§§§§§§§§§§§§§§

When Marie stepped out of the car at the spot where Dolla was, heads turned. Her half-shirt showed just enough skin, her bell bottoms hugged her curves perfectly, and her heels clicked against the pavement with authority. She walked past Dolla on purpose, her hips swaying, without looking at him until he called out.

"Yo, shorty," Dolla said, leaning against his car. His smile was smooth as silk. "What's your name?"

Marie turned slowly, giving him a once-over. "Depends. What's yours?"

"They call me Dolla," he said, stepping closer. "But you? You can call me Dupree."

Marie smirked. "Well, Dupree, I'm Marie."

Dupree's grin widened. "I know who you are."

Marie arched a brow. "Oh, you do?"

"Word travels fast," Dupree said, his voice low. "You James Loco's girl, right?

"Maybe I am. Maybe I'm not. What's it to you?"

Dupree chuckled, impressed by her boldness. "What you doing tonight?"

Marie tilted her head. "Whatever Dupree's doing."

Dupree laughed. "Let's ride."

"Let's!" Marie agreed.

"We riding with the top down too, so everybody can see us." Dupree sized Marie up biting his bottom lip. "They gonna hate to see Dupree and Marie. You think your homegirl will drive?"

"Of course she will." Marie felt a thrill shoot through her. She looked over making eye contact with Catherine.

"Of course I will. Let's ride!" Catherine said.

Chapter Twenty

Marie and Dupree

The night was electric. Dupree wasn't just smooth; he was charismatic, charming, and full of life. He and Marie rode through the city with the wind in their hair and the music blasting. Catherine drove up to a late-night diner, where they all laughed and talked like old friends. After they finished eating, Dupree dropped Catherine off at her car, and he and Marie continued to hang out.

When Dupree was finished hanging out, he pulled up to the Days Inn. He opened up the door to a presidential suite, where he and Marie settled on the couch, the TV flickering in the background.

"You something else, Marie," Dupree said, his arm draped over her shoulder.

"So are you," Marie replied, leaning into Dupree. They fell asleep like that, fully clothed, wrapped in each other's warmth.

What started as a revenge plan turned into something much more. Marie and Dupree were inseparable, and their chemistry was undeniable.

§§§§§§§§§§§§§§§§§§§§§§§§§§§§

By the next morning, word had spread. Asia found out about Dupree and Marie's ride, and she wasn't happy. She had a history of tracking down Dupree like she was the Secret Service, and today was one of those days. Asia stormed into the restaurant where Dupree and Marie were having brunch, her face twisted in rage.

"What the hell is this?" Asia shouted, pointing at them.

Dupree leaned back in his seat, unfazed. "Morning to you too, Asia."

"Don't 'morning' me!" Asia snapped, her voice shrill. She turned to Marie. "You think you can just show up and take my man?"

Marie set her coffee cup down calmly. "Funny. I thought you were busy chasing James Loco."

Asia's face turned crimson. "You don't know who you're messing with."

Marie leaned forward, her voice cold and steady. "Oh, I know exactly who I'm messing with. The question is, do you?"

Asia's face twisted with anger, but Marie didn't flinch.

"I refuse to be second to anyone," Marie proclaimed. "And to be clear when I step into someone's life, there is never room for competition. Dupree is not a fling. He's mine now. You can have James. He's history."

Chapter Twenty-One

James Return

Just when you thought things couldn't get any messier, James showed up at Marie's door later that evening.

"Marie, we need to talk," he said, his expression torn between guilt and desperation.

Marie crossed her arms. "Talk about what, James? About Asia? About your lies?"

James sighed. "I messed up, okay? But I love you. Asia doesn't mean anything to me."

Marie laughed bitterly. "Love me? You let some girl run her mouth in a salon about how she's riding in your car, you're so loyal, and she can't wait to spend time with you, and now you want to talk about love?"

James stepped closer. You know I love you! Marie leave Dolla alone! Please!"

"No, you listen, James. I don't do second place. And I definitely don't do lies. You think you can come here with some half-hearted apology and fix this? Boy, please."

James ran a hand over his face. "Marie, I swear it's not like that. I was just being stupid."

"Stupid doesn't cut it, James," Marie snapped. "Asia was running her mouth loud enough for a whole salon to hear. You didn't just mess up. You disrespected me."

James opened his mouth to respond, but before he could, a sleek car pulled up outside. The engine quiet, and the unmistakable figure of Dupree stepped out, leaning casually against the car as if he had all the time in the world.

Marie smirked. "Looks like you're about to meet someone new, James."

Dupree walked up to the door, his grin sharp and confident. "You good, Marie? Thought we were grabbing dinner."

James turned to Dupree, his eyes narrowing. "Who the hell is this?"

Dupree raised an eyebrow. "I'm Dolla. And you?"

"James," Marie interjected before James could answer, her voice dripping with sarcasm. "You know, the man who thought he could have his cake and eat it too."

James glared at Marie. "You're doing this just to get back at me."

Marie leaned against the doorframe; her expression cold. "You're right. At first, I was. But then I realized something. Dupree doesn't lie. He doesn't play games. And most importantly, he knows how to treat me."

Dupree chuckled, clearly enjoying the tension. "You heard the lady."

James clenched his fists, his face red with anger. "This isn't over, Marie."

"Oh, it's over," Marie said, her voice firm. "You just don't know it yet."

As James stormed off, Dupree turned to Marie, his grin softening into something almost tender. "You sure you're ready for all this drama, Marie?"

Marie shrugged. "Drama's just a part of life. But one thing's for sure, nobody plays me and walks away clean."

Dupree laughed, shaking his head. "You're something else, Marie."

"And don't you forget it," Marie said with a smirk, stepping into Dupree's car.

Chapter Twenty-Two
Asia's Revenge

Asia wasn't one to back down, and neither was James. The two of them started scheming together, their bruised egos fueling a plan to get back at Marie and Dupree.

Asia showed up at Dupree's usual spot one night, looking flawless and ready to cause trouble. "Hey, Dolla," she purred, sliding into the seat next to him. "Miss me?"

Dupree didn't even look up from his drink. "Nope, not even a little."

Asia laughed, but her eyes were sharp. "You think you can just run off and leave me in the dust? You're my man!"

Dupree finally looked at Asia, his expression bored. "Your man? Last time I checked, you were still chasing James."

Asia leaned closer, her voice dropping to a whisper. "You better watch yourself, Dolla. People like Marie don't stick around forever. And when she's gone, you'll come crawling back."

"Wishful thinking!" Dupree clapped back. "First of all, I don't crawl, and second, I will never be back!"

"We'll see! I'm gone!" Asia stormed away.

"Thank you and good-bye!" Dupree said with a smile.

Chapter Twenty-Three

Trouble Brewing

Meanwhile, James wasn't giving up either. He started showing up unannounced, trying to convince Marie to take him back.

One night, after getting the 411 on Dupree, James cornered Marie outside of her apartment. "Marie, you're making a big mistake. Dolla is not who you think he is."

Marie crossed her arms. "And you are? Please, James. Go back to Asia and leave me alone."

James shook his head, his voice desperate. "You don't know what you're getting into with him. Dolla's got a past, a dangerous one. People don't just walk away from someone like him."

Marie hesitated, her confidence wavering for the first time. But before she could respond, Dupree's car pulled up, and he stepped out, his expression unreadable.

"Everything okay here?" Dupree asked, his voice calm but laced with a quiet menace.

James glared at him. "Just telling Marie the truth. She deserves to know who she's dealing with."

Dupree smirked, his eyes cold. "The only thing Marie needs to know is that I take care of what's mine."

§§§§§§§§§§§§§§§§§§§§§§§§§§§§§§§§

The drama between James, Asia, Marie, and Dupree escalated into a tangled web of secrets, lies, and betrayal. As Marie dug deeper into Dupree's past, she discovered layers to him that both thrilled and terrified her.

Was Dupree really the man she thought he was? Or was James right about the danger lurking beneath the surface?

And as Asia and James's schemes grew bolder, Marie realized that the game she had started was spinning out of control.

The question was: would she survive it?

Chapter Twenty-Four
The Unraveling

Marie couldn't ignore James's warning, even though she hated to admit it might hold a kernel of truth. Dupree was smooth, charming, and undeniably magnetic, but there were cracks in his perfect facade. He'd disappear for days and hours, take mysterious phone calls, and shrug off her questions with that infuriating grin.

One night, Marie decided she needed answers. After Dupree left for "business," she called Catherine. "I need you to ride with me," Marie said, her voice tense.

Catherine hesitated. "Marie, are you sure about this? Dupree's got a reputation. People say he's not someone you want to cross."

Marie sighed. "I don't care about reputations. I care about the truth."

Catherine reluctantly agreed, and the two women tailed Dupree's car. He drove to a nondescript warehouse on the edge of town, where a group of men stood waiting. Marie's stomach tightened as she watched Dupree greet them with handshakes and laughter.

"Looks like a deal," Catherine whispered.

Marie frowned. "A deal for what, though?"

Before she could piece it together, the warehouse door swung open, and Dupree disappeared inside.

§§§§§§§§§§§§§§§§§§§§§§§§§§§§§§§

Later that night, Dupree returned to Marie's apartment, his face unreadable.

"Where were you?" Marie asked, her arms crossed.

Dupree smirked. "You asking as my girl or as my investigator?"

"Don't play games with me, Dupree," Marie snapped. "I followed you."

Duprees grin faltered, and for the first time, Marie saw something flicker in his eyes, anger, maybe even fear.

"You shouldn't have done that," Dupree said quietly.

"Why not?" Marie demanded. "What are you hiding?"

Dupree stepped closer, his voice low and intense. "Marie, there are parts of my life you don't need to know about. For your own safety."

"Safety?" Marie scoffed. "What, are you in the mafia now? Running a drug ring? You a killer? What is it, Dupree?"

Dupree grabbed Marie's hands, his grip firm but not harsh. "Listen to me. I would never let anything happen to you. But you have to trust me."

Marie pulled away, her heart pounding. "Trust? How can I trust you when you're keeping secrets?"

Chapter Twenty-Five

Asia's Betrayal

While Marie wrestled with her doubts, Asia was busy plotting. She'd caught wind of Marie's snooping and decided it was the perfect opportunity to strike. One afternoon, she showed up at Marie's job, her smile sugary sweet but her eyes full of malice.

"Can we talk?" Asia asked.

Marie rolled her eyes. "We don't have anything to talk about."

"Oh, I think we do," Asia said, leaning in. "You see, Dolla and I go way back. And he's not as clean as you think."

Marie forced a laugh. "You must be desperate, Asia."

Asia smirked. "Desperate? No. Informed? Yes. Ask Dupree about 'the deal', the one at the warehouse last night." Marie froze, her confidence cracking. Asia noticed and leaned closer. "You think you're special, but you're just another player in his game. And when it falls apart, don't say I didn't warn you."

When Marie left she was disappointed and confused and could not wait to see Dupree.

Marie confronted Dupree again that night, this time armed with Asia's accusations.

"Who are you, really?" Marie demanded.

Dupree sighed, running a hand through his hair. "Marie, I've tried to protect you from this. But if you really want the truth, fine. I run with people who… handle things like business deals, debts, enforcement, and things that are off the record or under the radar."

"So, it's true. You're a criminal." Marie said.

Dupree met Marie's gaze, his expression unapologetic. "Wow! No, I'm not a criminal. I've done what I had to do. But none of it changes how I feel about you."

"How can I be with someone I can't even trust?" Marie whispered.

Dupree stepped closer, his voice soft. "Because you know I'd never hurt you. And because I make you feel alive."

Marie was torn between her feelings for Dupree and the chaos that surrounded him. But before she could make a decision, James and Asia launched their final plan.

They tipped off the authorities about Dupree's dealings, and one night, his world came crashing down. Marie watched in horror as police swarmed Dupree's usual hangout, arresting him and his crew.

Dupree locked eyes with Marie as they put him in cuffs. "I'll be back, Marie. This isn't over."

As he was led away, Marie's heart shattered. But deep down, she knew Dupree was right. Their story wasn't over, it was just beginning.

And as Marie turned to leave, she couldn't shake the feeling that she was walking straight into another storm, one she might not survive.

Chapter Twenty-Six

The Redemption of Dupree

People love to judge a book by its cover, and Dupree's cover? It was messy, dramatic, and riddled with mistakes. But beneath all the chaos, I saw a man with potential, a man worth saving, even if he didn't know it yet. Our start and where we are now is deep.

I wasn't blind to the trouble Dupree brought into my life. Women calling my phone at all hours, jealous exes showing up uninvited, and his frequent trips to jail for things I told him were beneath him. But when I love, I love hard. And when I saw something in Dupree that no one else could, I wasn't about to give up on him.

When Dupree got arrested on those bogus charges, I knew something wasn't right. That wasn't the man I knew. He had his flaws, sure, but Dupree wasn't reckless. He'd been set up. James and Asia's handiwork, I had no doubt.

That's when I decided I wasn't just going to sit back and watch the system eat Dupree alive. Lucky for him, I had connections. My good friend, Shela Renee Johnston, had just been appointed to head prosecutor in our district. If anyone could help me get Dupree a fair shake, it was her.

When I walked into Shela's office, I laid it all out: "Look, Shela, I'm not saying Dupree is an angel. But he's not guilty of this. I've got the proof, and I need you to help me give him a second chance. He's got too much potential to let this be the end of his story."

Shela leaned back in her chair, studying me. "Marie, you always did have a thing for fixing broken people. Are you sure this man is worth the risk?"

I didn't hesitate. "He's more than worth it."

Dupree got two years of unsupervised probation. In the world we lived in, that was practically a miracle. When I told Dupree the news during our jailhouse visit, he looked at me with a mix of disbelief and gratitude.

"You did this for me?" he asked, his voice barely above a whisper.

"Of course I did," I said, my tone firm. "But this is it, Dupree. No more excuses, no more getting caught up in the streets. You're too smart, too good for this life. You've got to build something real out here, for yourself and for us."

Dupree nodded, but I could see the doubt in his eyes. That's when I looked him straight in the eyes.

"You are more than this, Dupree," I said. "You're not just some street king with a fast car and a flashy life. You're a man with heart, a man who could be so much more if you'd just see it for yourself. I need you to see it, Dupree. Because I do."

"I don't know why you put up with me." Dupree responded.

I laughed softly. "Because I know your worth, Dupree. And one day, you're going to know it too."

Chapter Twenty-Seven
Let's Go Back
Pact - 1992

Before we left for college in 1992, Marcellus and I made a pact, no matter how far apart, we'd keep our love strong. We weren't about outside distractions; we wanted to build what we had. At least, that's what we believed. Trust was there, but we underestimated the dangers of distance. Without each other's physical comfort, we stepped into uncharted territory, blind to the realities that could test our faithfulness and loyalty.

We thought love alone could shield us from the impossibilities, but life had other plans. Marcellus and I love each other deeply, there's no question about that. But now, we're left wondering: will our love stand the test of time, or will the distance become a battle we can't win?

This isn't just some sappy love story; it's raw, emotional, and real. We're riding this out like soldiers, gangster in our loyalty, but tender in our hearts. No matter what, our love will either survive the storm or shatter under the pressure. Either way, we're in this together, fighting for what we have.

Chapter Twenty-Eight
Crossroads - 1994

Marcellus and I had made the decision to attend different universities. He went off to the University of Oklahoma, and I stayed closer to home at the University of Nebraska in Lincoln. I liked being just an hour away from home, able to visit my family whenever I wanted. We promised to maintain our long-distance relationship, and for a while, everything seemed perfect. Marcellus would come home during holidays, and we'd spend a lot of our time together. Life was good. I excelled in my classes and made it to the Dean's List, and Marcellus thrived as the star quarterback.

But college brought new experiences and new people. At Nebraska, I met Cedric, a tall, intelligent junior from a wealthy family. He was charming and attentive, but while he seemed to be falling for me, my heart was still with Marcellus. I enjoyed Cedric's company, but I made it clear that my feelings didn't run as deep as his.

Unbeknownst to me, Marcellus was living a double life. At Oklahoma, he had a girlfriend, Vanessa, a wealthy girl whose family supported him. Vanessa was the picture of privilege, providing Marcellus with everything he needed. To his friends and teammates, she was his girlfriend, but back home, I was the one he professed his love to.

One day, feeling spontaneous and wanting to surprise Marcellus, I decided to visit him in Oklahoma. I dressed to impress, cute bell bottoms, stylish heels, and my hair flowing perfectly. I brought flowers and a card to congratulate him on his success. Excitedly, I knocked on his dorm room door.

To my surprise, a girl opened the door, a white girl with a valley accent. "Who are you?" she asked, confused.

"I'm here for Marcellus," I said confidently. "I'm his girlfriend."

She smirked. "I am Vanessa. You're looking for my boyfriend, Marcellus? Come in."

I followed her inside, my heart pounding. There, in the room, stood Marcellus, wrapped in a towel, frozen in shock when he saw me.

"Marie," he stammered, "what are you doing here?"

"What do you mean, what am I doing here? I'm here to surprise my boyfriend. But clearly, I'm the one surprised," I said, my voice trembling with a mix of anger and hurt.

Vanessa interjected, her tone dripping with disdain. "Marcellus, care to explain who this is? I've done everything for you, and this is how you repay me?"

Vanessa turned to me, her voice sharp. "He's just a poor boy from the projects, using me for everything. And you, what are you? Another distraction?"

Marie struggled to hold back her anger when Vanessa belittled Marcellus, calling him just a poor boy from the projects who was using her for everything. The blatant disrespect stung, but Marie decided to bite her tongue. Since Marcellus remained silent, she chose to let it go, thinking they could discuss it later in private. Marcellus, clearly torn, knew he had a tough decision to make.

Marie finally shot back, "I'm Marie, and I'm far from just a distraction. Marcellus, you need to tell her the truth. Who am I to you? Because this isn't what we agreed on."

Marcellus stood there, torn and speechless. "Marie," he finally said, "you know I care about you. We've been through so much together, but…"

"No buts, Marcellus," I cut him off. "You lied to me. You made me believe I was your only one, while you were playing house with Vanessa. I came here out of love, and I find this mess?"

Vanessa crossed her arms. "Yeah, Marcellus, explain yourself. Who am I to you? Because I deserve the truth."

Marcellus looked between us, his face a mix of guilt and confusion. The web of lies was unraveling, and he could no longer hide. It was time for him to choose, to face the consequences of his actions. No more lies. No more games. This was the moment of reckoning.

Taking a deep breath, Marcellus finally spoke. "Marie, I'm so sorry. I love you, and we've shared so much together. You've been my best friend for years, but Vanessa is my girlfriend. She's the one I'm with, and she's the one I choose. I hate that you had to find out this way, and I should have handled it differently."

Marie felt the weight of Marcellus' words hit her like a ton of bricks. Her heart ached, but she kept her composure. "I understand, Marcellus," Marie said, her voice steady but strained. "Congratulations, Vanessa. You've got a great guy here, and I hope he treats you right. I wish you both the best."

With that, Marie turned and walked away, with her head held high. She knew she couldn't let them see the pain she felt. She had always been taught to never show weakness and to leave with dignity no matter the circumstances. But as soon as she was out of sight, the tears streamed down her face, silently releasing the heartbreak she carried as she left the campus.

Chapter Twenty-Nine
Queen Marie

Marie was a whirlwind of emotions, hurt, broken, distraught, angry, and confused all at once. The betrayal she felt was unlike anything she had ever experienced. Marcellus had blindsided her, publicly choosing another girl, Vanessa, over her. Not just any girl, a rich, white, privileged girl who had belittled him, calling him "just a poor boy from the projects." Yet, despite the humiliation, Marcellus stood by Vanessa. The trust Marie had in him shattered into pieces.

Marie had planned to stay with Marcellus, but now she was left to fend for herself. She booked a room at the nearest Hampton Inn, where she collapsed into darkness, with the weight of her pain pressing down on her. She cried, screamed, and questioned everything.

"How could Marcellus do this to me?"

Marie's phone buzzed, Cedric was calling. She let it go to voicemail, realizing she couldn't face anyone right now. But then it hit her. Marie realized she had someone back home who adored her, yet her heart still ached for Marcellus.

Caught in a web of confusion, Marie prayed for clarity, pleading for a sign. She changed her flight to leave early in the morning, determined to escape this nightmare. Just as she was about to sink deeper into despair, her phone rang again. It was Marcellus. Hesitant, she answered. His voice, filled with remorse, poured through the line.

"Marie, I'm so sorry. I had to say those things to keep things stable. Vanessa's family is my ticket to a future. They believe in me and invest in me, but it's all for their gain. I need them to help me finish school, but you are my heart. You are everything to me. Please understand, this is temporary. You and I, we're forever. Can I see you, please?"

Marie's heart twisted with conflicting emotions. She wanted to stay mad, and cut Marcellus off, but his words reached a part of her that still believed in their bond. She agreed to see Marcellus, so he came to her room. When he arrived with roses and apologies, Marie let him explain further. Marie had no idea that Marcellus' future career was at stake, and Vanessa's wealthy family provided the support and resources that she couldn't offer. His ambition, his dreams, he was caught in a situation where love and survival clashed. Marie listened, and despite her pain, she understood.

In that moment, Marie transformed. She realized she could endure this, not as a victim, but as a queen who understood the game being played. She held her head high, kissed Marcellus, and accepted the reality with a fierce determination. This wasn't her defeat; it was a step in their journey. Marcellus needed her strength, and she would give it, but on her terms.

That night, for the first time, Marie and Marcellus came together, their connection deepening as they shared an intimate love, born from the trials they had faced. It was a profound moment, solidifying a bond forged in adversity, a connection so strong, it felt unbreakable.

As Marie walked away the next day, she carried herself like a boss, her spirit unshaken. She knew who she was, and no one could take that from her. She would let Marcellus navigate his path, but she was no one's fool. She was the queen of her own story, and she would always rise.

Chapter Thirty
Street Smart

All this drama and confusion started to click for Marie. It was like a lightbulb went off, and suddenly she got it. Her parents had been trying to school her on this game from the jump. Her dad always told her to keep her cool, stay grounded, and never let love blind her. Her mom warned her about giving too much of herself too soon, about keeping her guard up, and watching people's actions, not just their words. They were dropping knowledge to prepare her for moments like this, and now, it all made sense.

Marie realized she needed to play it smart, not emotional. Love was cool, but friendship was the foundation. Don't dive in headfirst, stay back, watch, and move with caution. You could be friends without getting your heart all tangled up. You could be in a relationship, but only if it was solid, only if the other person proved they were worth it. This wasn't about getting caught up in fairy tales; it was about Marie keeping her power, and her sense of self intact.

Marie understood now that she had to love from a distance, keep her emotions in check, and never lose herself over anyone. Her parents had been right all along. The game was about control, about not letting anyone play you. Marie was growing into a boss, someone who could navigate relationships without losing her cool, without losing herself. She would tread lightly, peep game, and let actions speak louder than words.

From here on out, Marie knew she had to stay sharp, stay in control, and never let her heart lead her into a trap. She was learning the art of the game, and she was going to master it. This was about survival, about making sure she never got played again. Marie was stepping into her power, and from now on, she'd be the one calling the shots.

Chapter Thirty-One
A Visit With Mom and Dad

Marie, feeling a wave of emotions, made her way back home and went to visit her dad. As they sat together, she opened up about the emotional roller coasters she had been riding in her love life. She reflected on the lessons her father had instilled in her, about staying grounded and always keeping her head on a swivel when it came to men. At that moment, she truly grasped the wisdom behind her dad's words. She realized that his guidance wasn't just about being cautious but about understanding her own worth and navigating relationships with clarity and strength. This newfound understanding brought a sense of peace and gratitude, knowing her dad's advice was rooted in protecting her heart and helping her recognize red flags before they became emotional scars.

Afterward, Marie called her mom to share her appreciation. With a warm tone, she thanked her mother for always keeping it real with her and never sugarcoating the truth. She opened up about Marcellus, hinting at the lessons she had learned from that experience. Marie now understood the profound difference between friendship and loyalty. Her mother had always emphasized that while faithfulness was important, loyalty held a deeper, more enduring value. Loyalty wasn't just about staying committed but about standing by someone through thick and thin, with unwavering support and trust. For the first time, Marie truly saw why loyalty surpassed faithfulness. It was about being there in spirit and action, even when the world turned upside down. This realization deepened her appreciation for the bonds that truly mattered, and she felt a newfound respect for the life lessons her mother had imparted.

Chapter Thirty-Two
Valentine's Day – 1996

Dupree was on a remarkable streak of consistency lately, and I couldn't be prouder of him. Life hasn't been kind to him. He's faced obstacles since he was just 10, in and out of jail, always battling a system that seemed determined to keep him down. But now, things are different. Dupree hasn't been in trouble for a while, and I see the strength in him every day. Despite the whispers and sideways glances, despite his past haunting him like a shadow, Dupree is carving out a better path.

People have their opinions about him, warning me to stay away, to be cautious. "He's dangerous," they say. "He'll hurt you." But they don't know Dupree like I do. Beneath the tough exterior is a man who cares deeply. With me, he's gentle, kind, and real. Our connection is raw and genuine. He knows I care, truly care, and that brings out the best in him.

This Valentine's Day feels extra special. I've planned an unforgettable evening for us, a night of laughter, love, and new experiences. Dupree has never heard of Hibachi, and when I mentioned it, he gave me the cutest, puzzled look and asked, "What language is that?" I couldn't help but laugh. His innocence in moments like these melts my heart.

The excitement bubbled within me as I got ready. I chose the perfect outfit, a stunning red one-piece with an off-the-shoulder design that felt both elegant and flirty. The diamond accents shimmered, matching the sparkly earrings that dangled with every movement. I knew tonight was going to be magical, and I wanted to look as special as the night felt.

When we finally met at the restaurant, it was like the world faded away. Dupree walked in, and his eyes lit up as he saw me. The energy between us was electric, filled with anticipation and joy. I handed him a rose and a heartfelt card, watching his face soften with a smile that was just for me. He handed over a beautiful bouquet of chocolate-covered fruit from Edible Arrangements.

The evening unfolded beautifully. We laughed, we talked, and we shared moments that felt like pure magic. The Hibachi experience was new for Dupree, and seeing his delight with each sizzling dish brought me so much happiness. The way he looked at me, the way he made me feel, everything was perfect.

In that moment, surrounded by the warmth of our connection, I knew this was exactly where I wanted to be. Dupree and I were living in our own little world, filled with love, laughter, and promise. This Valentine's Day wasn't just special; it was unforgettable. I couldn't help but feel that this was just the beginning of something truly extraordinary.

Chapter Thirty-Three
Quit Playing

And just like clockwork, in my good moment, Cedric showed up looking sharp as a tack, dressed to impress, with a smug grin and a pretty young thang clinging to his arm. They were matching outfits from head to toe, coordinated down to the color scheme. I couldn't help but laugh to myself. "Matching outfits? Either they're in love, or it's brand new, because seriously, who does that?" I was amused by the cliché of it all.

Cedric spotted me, and with that trademark swagger of his, he strolled over, trying to be cute and playful. He nudged me with his elbow and said, "Hey Marie," like this was the moment for that, or it was cool or something.

I didn't skip a beat. "Hey Cedric. This is Dupree," I said with a smooth confidence, my voice carrying just enough edge to make it clear that I was not here for any nonsense.

Dupree, cool and collected, extended a hand. "What's up, man?" he said, giving Cedric a casual dap, his demeanor unbothered but alert.

Cedric's smirk faltered for a moment, and his confusion flickered across his face as he glanced at Dupree. He mumbled something under his breath and walked away without so much as introducing the girl clinging to his arm. She stood there awkwardly for a second, clearly uncomfortable, before following Cedric like a shadow.

Cedric thought he was being funny, pulling some sort of power move, but I saw right through it. I wasn't about to let him play games, not with me, and definitely not with Dupree. I watched him retreat with that smug look on his face, but he knew better.

I was always a step ahead. I am not one to leave things to chance or give anyone room to question me or my relationship. I introduced Dupree with pride, and treated Cedric like he was an old classmate or a distant cousin. It was all about keeping things classy and under control. Drama and messiness? That's just not my style. No one was going to have the chance to think they could play me, not Cedric, not anyone.

I shut it down effortlessly, the silent message clear: Dupree is my man, and I wasn't about to let anyone, especially Cedric, stir up trouble or throw shade our way. As Cedric and his girl slinked off, the embarrassment clung to them like a second skin; I stood tall, allowing my presence to radiate strength and confidence.

Dupree glanced at me with a subtle smile on his face. He didn't need words to express his appreciation; I had made it crystal clear that he was my priority, and I had his back, no matter what.

As the night continued, the tension from Cedric's little stunt faded into the background. Me and Dupree were unbothered, enjoying each other's company, leaving no room for the petty drama Cedric tried to bring. And while Cedric and his pretty young thing faded into the crowd, Me and Dupree remained the real stars of the night, untouchable, unstoppable, and unshakable.

Chapter Thirty-Four
Grow Up

So, picture this: Besides that one sort of setback, Cedric, we were having the perfect evening. We were done eating and waiting for our food to be put in to-go containers. We tipped our cook because he absolutely killed it with the tricks and service. The night was smooth, everything was on point, and just when I thought it couldn't get any better, bam, in walks a situation I didn't see coming.

A grown woman, and I mean grown, steps into the place. I'm talking older than 30, older than 40… she might've been pushing my parents' age. And she wasn't alone, oh no, she had her kids in tow. The hostess was leading her to her section as we were getting ready to leave ours, and this woman? She stops, dead in her tracks, and makes a beeline for me and Dupree.

"Excuse me, kids, look who it is!" She says, loud enough for the whole restaurant to hear. "Look, he's got a rose and a card. And who is this? Is this your sister, Dolla?"

I mean, really? Sister? Dupree kept it calm, but I could feel the heat rising. "No, this is Marie. This is my girl. Why are you tripping?"

"Oh, your girl?" she shoots back, eyes wide. "Look, kids, Dolla's got a girl. Isn't that special?" She was really putting on a show now.

I'm sitting there, stunned, but I'm not about to let this slide. "I'm Marie," I say, cutting through the noise. "What's up?"

"Oh, I'm Rochelle. And he's talking about his girl? I thought I was his girl," she starts in, her voice dripping with sarcasm and hurt. "Because, you know, I see this man every day. I've got a household full of his things. He pays the bills at the house we live in. Two names on the lease, mine and his. And this ring?" She flashes a ring in Dupree's face. "I thought this meant something."

Dupree stays cool, but I can tell even he's over this nonsense. "Rochelle, I bought you that ring because you liked it. It was a gift. It's just a ring! Why are you tripping? I'm here with my girl. Relax."

But Rochelle? She wasn't having it. "You think this is a game? What does this ring mean, Dolla?"

And I'm just sitting there, watching this unfold, thinking how ridiculous it all is. This woman's got her kids with her, and she's putting on this circus in public? Really?

"You know what?" I say, calm but firm. "You came here with your kids. Why don't you go eat with them and stop acting up? You're supposed to be an adult."

She shoots me a glare. "How old are you, little girl?"

But by then, she's realized she's made enough of a fool of herself. She takes her kids and finally walks away. Good thing, too, because I was just getting warmed up.

I mean, really. We were just trying to have a good Valentine's Day, and here comes this drama queen, dragging her kids into her mess. Dupree can't even enjoy himself without someone popping up trying to stir the pot. But she saw me. Oh, she saw me, me and all my cuteness, and she knew. Whatever she thought she had? It was nothing. She knew it, and so did I.

And that's how the night ended. A perfect evening flipped into chaos because Dupree's always got someone out there who can't keep their act together. But guess what? I stay cute, stay classy, and keep it moving. Drama queens can try, but they never win.

Chapter Thirty-Five
Congratulations - 1996

Marie and Marcellus's graduations were nothing short of remarkable, a celebration of perseverance, hard work, and the unbreakable bond they shared. Marie beamed with pride as she walked across the stage to receive her Master of Science in Counseling, with a concentration in Clinical Mental Health Counseling, from the University of Nebraska Omaha. Her heart swelled with joy knowing she was now equipped to make a profound difference in people's lives.

Marcellus, equally proud, stood tall as he was handed his Master of Arts in Athletic Training, achieving a stunning 3.920 GPA. The auditorium roared with applause, a testament to his dedication not just to academics but to his lifelong passion for sports. Both of them had navigated the complexities of graduate school while managing life's outside demands, a feat that didn't go unnoticed by their supportive families and friends.

In May, Marie had her graduation, where Marcellus stood front and center, cheering her on with all his heart. A month later, it was Marcellus's turn, and Marie was there, not front and center, but in the background because of Marcellus' circumstances. Her pride for him was evident in her shining eyes. Each had become a pillar of support for the other, their bond unshakeable despite the challenges at hand and ahead.

Marcellus and Marie basked in the glow of their achievements. Their dreams were unfolding, their futures bright, and in this moment, surrounded by love and triumph, they knew that no matter the distance, their hearts would always remain intertwined.

The air buzzed with excitement as they celebrated. Marie's family embraced her with joyful tears, while Marcellus's parents clapped with pride, their son's accomplishments shining brightly. Their friends, many of whom had shared the academic journey with them, cheered loudly, reveling in the mutual triumph.

Despite their incredible achievements, a bittersweet undertone lingered. Marie's heart was heavy with the thought of Marcellus moving to Pittsburgh, drafted as a first-round quarterback for the Steelers. She knew their paths were diverging, and the thought of being apart from her best friend even longer tugged at her soul. Marcellus felt it too, the weight of impending distance between them, but for now, they focused on the joy of the present moment.

Marie and Marcellus were on the cusp of greatness. Marie ready to make her mark in mental health counseling at Bergen Mercy, and Marcellus gearing up for the NFL stage. They were proud, hopeful, and deeply connected, their friendship a cornerstone of their strength. This was their time, and they embraced it with open hearts, knowing that their future held endless possibilities.

Chapter Thirty-Six
Lunch Date – 1997

The day started off on a high note, as Marie woke up with a smile, knowing the day could only get better. Just as she was soaking in the good vibes, Cedric, the valedictorian-turned-billionaire investor, reached out with an invite to a luxurious candlelight lunch at his sprawling mansion in Ranch View Estates, Omaha. The buzz around town was that Cedric had secured the biggest and best house on the block, and Marie was curious to see it for herself.

Cedric, still the charming guy from their past, had transformed into a business strategist, author, public speaker, and the voice behind the most popular radio show in the world, Real LOVE Works. Despite his success, Cedric remained single, but his reputation with women preceded him, seven and a half kids with eight baby mamas. Marie wasn't looking for a stepmother role, but a peek at that mansion? Why not. Plus, she and Cedric were still cool, and she wasn't committed to anyone.

Cedric's house, which was everything everyone was bragging about, totally wowed Marie. It was luxury and elegance all in one. This immaculate two-story house had seven spacious bedrooms, seven bathrooms with glass tile flooring that gleamed under the natural light, and a three-car garage. There was also a massive swimming pool that shimmered in the sunlight in the backyard.

The lunch was everything one could expect from Cedric, lavish and refined. Steak, shrimp, baked potatoes, and asparagus filled the air with mouthwatering aromas. Cedric, the showman, sported a Versace shirt with the top buttons teasingly undone, fancy dress pants, and gleaming shoes, all topped off with Gucci cologne. His new piercings, a left ear, eyebrow, chin, and tongue, added an unexpected edge, complementing his perfectly tapered low afro and clean baby face. This wasn't the boy Marie once knew; Cedric was now a grown man.

Marie arrived looking stunning in a short dress that showcased her legs with her feet gracefully adorned in open-toe sandals. Their conversation flowed effortlessly, touching on their future aspirations. After lunch, they lounged on the couch, laughing at the movie

House Party. Cedric saw his chance to finally close the gap between them, craving a moment of closeness he hadn't dared to reach for before.

Just as the moment seemed ripe, Marie's phone buzzed. The caller ID was unknown, but the voice on the other end was unmistakable. "Hello, Marie, your one and only is out!" It was Dupree. The excitement in her voice was evident, and Cedric noticed.

"Who's that?" Cedric asked, his curiosity irritated.

Marie, caught up in her joy, barely registered Cedric's question. "It's Dupree. He's out!" she exclaimed.

Dupree was finally free after a dramatic legal battle. He had been jailed for standing up for a woman being abused in a nightclub, a decision that cost him his freedom but showcased his integrity. Despite the obstacles, including a vindictive prosecutor, Dupree's charges were dropped after the victim finally came forward.

Marie had no hesitation. "Cedric, I have to go. Dupree's home."

Cedric, though disappointed, understood the weight of Dupree's return. "We had a good time, Marie. I'm thankful for tonight."

Marie smiled, "Lunch was amazing, Cedric. You're the sweetest guy ever, and I hope we can do this again." She hugged him tightly, but Cedric, feeling the sting of rejection, barely reciprocated.

As Marie walked out, Cedric was left reflecting on what could have been. He knew when Dupree called, everything else faded into the background.

Chapter Thirty-Seven

Drama Life

Marie couldn't believe how amazing her day had been with Dupree. They had finally found a moment to truly connect. For Marie, it felt like a dream—the kind of perfect day she'd longed for since meeting Dupree a couple of years ago. The two of them had spent hours together, laughing, sharing stories, and enjoying each other's company. They cruised through the city, visited some of Dupree's favorite spots, stopped at a local diner to indulge in some comfort food, and even stopped by the mall. Marie was on cloud nine, thrilled to finally be spending quality time with Dupree.

For the first time, Dupree opened up his world to Marie. He introduced her to a few of his friends and even his grandmother, something he had never done before. Dupree was always secretive, preferring to keep his personal life separate. But today felt different. He explained to Marie that he had kept her away from his life's chaos to protect her, wanting to shield her from any trouble he might be involved in. Marie appreciated his honesty, feeling special and cherished.

As they strolled through the mall, Dupree decided they should do some shopping. The atmosphere was light and carefree. But just as Marie thought nothing could spoil their day, a woman approached them with a tense expression.

"What are you doing, Dolla?" the woman snapped, standing too close for comfort.

Dupree's smile faded as he responded coolly, "What are you doing in my face?"

Marie stood by, letting Dupree handle the situation, though ready to step in if needed.

The woman's voice sharpened, "I'm trying to figure out when you came home. You didn't even tell me."

Dupree remained calm but firm, "Why do you need to know? We're not connected like that."

The woman's eyes narrowed. "Not connected? Just because you happen to be with this broad don't get to acting funny. I was the one you called from jail, the one you leaned on. Every time you needed someone, it was me."

Marie, maintaining her composure, interjected, "Excuse me, I'm not a 'broad.' I'm Marie, Marie Tucker. Keep it respectful!"

The woman backed down slightly, mumbling an apology underneath her breath, but the damage was done.

Dupree tried to dismiss the woman, but she had one final bombshell: "You see this baby bump? It's yours. Now are we connected?" The woman walked away, looking back and smiling at Marie.

Marie's heart sank as the woman's words hung in the air. Dupree, visibly uncomfortable, tried to brush it off, leading Marie away. "Come on, Marie. Let's go." They walked away right out through the exit door.

Just when Marie thought it couldn't get any worse, another woman approached Dupree as they left the mall. "Hey, Dolla! Didn't know you had a girl. You're a trip."

Marie, now frustrated and exhausted, confronted the woman. "Look, we're just trying to have a good time. If you want to speak, speak. But keep it respectful. Dupree doesn't belong to anyone but himself, and right now, he's with me."

As the other woman backed off, Marie turned to Dupree, her voice firm but steady. "This is not what I signed up for, Dupree. I won't be disrespected. You better teach your girls to shut that mouth when you are with me. My guys would never do you like that! They know better."

Dupree stayed quiet and unlocked the car. The drive home was filled with silence, and the joy from earlier moments had completely evaporated. Marie's mind raced, trying to process the whirlwind of emotions. Dupree's reassurances fell flat, and the weight of the unexpected drama was too much to ignore.

Marie, don't let this ruin us please," Dupree pleaded.

Marie looked out the window, her voice barely above a whisper. "I just need time to think."

The once-perfect day had taken a dramatic turn, leaving Marie to question everything. The joy, the laughter, the connection, they were now overshadowed by secrets and revelations. Yet, despite the chaos, something inside her still held on, hoping that maybe, just maybe, they could find their way back to each other.

§§§§§§§§§§§§§§§§§§§§§§§§§§§§§§§§

Marie called Catherine. "Where you at?" Marie questioned when Catherine answered her phone.

"I am at home. Me and Tasha are just sitting here talking," Catherine responded.

"I'm on my way over there, and I need to talk now." Marie put her phone back in her purse. "Please take me to 2578 Pratt Street." Marie continued looking out the window quietly.

"Ok!" Dupree answered, disappointed with himself.

Chapter Thirty-Eight

The Talk

Marie knocked on Catherine's door with a force that matched the storm brewing inside her. Catherine opened the door, her face lighting up before she noticed the tension in Marie's eyes.

"What's up, Girl? You sounded stressed. What's going on?" Catherine asked, pulling her friend inside.

Tasha, lounging on the couch, looked up. "Yeah, Girl. Spill the tea."

Marie shook her head, her voice trembling. "No, this is not tea, Honey. This is not tea. Don't treat my situation like tea. This is real, Girl."

Catherine and Tasha exchanged concerned glances. "What happened?" Catherine pressed.

Marie sighed deeply, her voice heavy with frustration. "You are not going to believe it when I tell you. So, I was hanging with Dupree."

"Dupree?" Catherine's eyebrows shot up.

"Yeah, Dupree?" Tasha echoed, leaning forward.

Marie nodded, her voice rising with emotion. "Yeah, he got out."

"Oh God," Tasha muttered, shaking her head. "I knew he went to jail. He's been in there for so many months, always back and forth. It's always something."

"That don't even matter," Marie snapped, pacing the room. "Listen. We were at the mall, having a good time. Then, this girl runs up. She starts going off, talking about how Dupree's been calling her from jail, and now he's out, and she's hearing nothing. She even had the nerve to say, 'This baby bump is yours.'"

Catherine gasped, covering her mouth. "She's pregnant?"

"By Dupree, apparently. And let me tell you, she made sure I saw that bump. Poked it out like she was showcasing it."

"Marie," Catherine said gently. "I know you ain't tripping; I mean, you were with him. He chose to be with you."

Tasha chimed in, her tone firm. "Exactly. He was with you, not her. She's just mad because she didn't get the call."

Marie's voice wavered, tears threatening to spill. "But he didn't call me either while he was in jail. I didn't hear from him at all."

Tasha sighed. "Girl, do you know how expensive those jail calls are? You need to have an understanding with someone before you just call them from jail."

Marie straightened, with a bold spark in her eyes. "We have an understanding. Dupree is my person."

Tasha chuckled, "Well, you need to remember that when you're feeling all this because he's showing you where his heart is."

Catherine nodded, stepping closer. "Marie, don't let that shake you. Dupree showed her that he's with you."

Marie bit her lip, her mind racing. "I just feel disrespected. No one ever steps to me like that. Dupree needs to handle his business."

Catherine placed a comforting hand on Marie's shoulder. "Listen, Girl. You're letting this get to you too much. You know Dupree loves you. You know he respects you."

Marie's defenses started to crumble. "You think?"

Catherine smiled. "I know. And you love him too. So, stop letting these other girls mess with your peace. Focus on what you have."

Marie exhaled, her tension easing. "You're right. I do love him. I just…I hope he calls me. I'm not calling him, though."

"You could call him," Catherine suggested with a sly grin.

Marie laughed through her tears. "Maybe, but right now, I just need a sign from God."

At that moment, Marie's phone rang. She stared at it, the room falling silent. Slowly, she picked it up, her heart pounding.

Catherine and Tasha exchanged knowing smiles. "There's your sign, Girl."

Marie couldn't help but smile, her heart filling with hope.

Chapter Thirty-Nine

Happy Now

"Hey there, Sunshine," a deep, sexy voice spoke through the phone as Marie answered.

Marie froze, her heart leaping in her chest. "Marcellus?" she whispered, hardly believing her ears.

"I miss you, my Marie," Marcellus said, a smile evident in his voice.

Marie's hand flew to her mouth as a gasp escaped. "Oh my God, Marcellus! Are you kidding me? I miss you so much! You don't even understand what this call means to me."

Across the room, Tasha and Catherine were silently cheering, exchanging high fives. "It's Marcellus!" Catherine mouthed with wide eyes.

"I need you to do me a favor," Marcellus continued smoothly. "I bought you a ticket for my game tomorrow. Your flight leaves at 9:00 AM. The game isn't until 6:20 PM, but I need to see you there."

"Wait, what?" Marie stammered, her head spinning. "You're moving too fast, Marcellus!"

Marcellus chuckled softly, his voice comforting. "Listen, Baby, I can't talk tonight. The team is doing some last-minute bonding before we win this Super

Bowl tomorrow. I've got to go. See you tomorrow, my Marie." And with that, Marcellus hung up.

Marie stared at her phone, stunned, before letting out an excited scream. "You guys are not going to believe this! Marcellus bought me a ticket to his game tomorrow. I'm flying out in the morning! He said he needs to see me!"

Catherine grinned. "That is definitely a sign."

"Omg, what a sign!" Tasha added, shaking her head in disbelief. "I knew you talked about Marcellus, but I didn't realize you two were still like that. I mean, I just acted like I knew, but for real?"

Marie shot Tasha a look, half-laughing. "Girl, do I lie? Of course, it's for real!"

Tasha laughed, her voice echoing through the room. "I mean, Marcellus is a global superstar, but you, you're just an Omaha boss!"

"Girl, shut up!" Marie yelled playfully, swatting at Tasha.

Catherine leaned in, her eyes sparkling with excitement. "What are you going to do?"

Marie's face lit up with determination. "I'm going to the game."

"I knew it!" Catherine exclaimed. "Wow, this is huge!"

Marie glanced at the clock, her mind racing. "Okay, I gotta go. Catherine, you know I'm not driving. Can you take me home?"

"Of course…" Catherine began, but she was interrupted by a knock at the door.

Chapter Forty

Forgive Me Please

Catherine walked to the door with curiosity etched on her face. As she opened the door, Marie's heart skipped a beat, and her eyes widened in shock.

Standing there was Dupree, his expression a mix of determination and vulnerability. "Hey, Dupree," Catherine greeted softly, stepping aside. "Come in." Dupree nodded, stepping inside with purpose. His eyes immediately found Marie, and the room seemed still. "Thank you, Catherine," Dupree said quietly before turning his full attention to Marie. "I just need to talk to you."

Marie's heart raced, her mind spinning with questions. Dupree took a few steps closer, his voice filled with emotion. "Marie, I'm sorry. I'm so sorry for everything that happened today. I never intended for you to get hurt, but you did, and I need you to know how deeply I regret it."

Dupree paused, his eyes searching Marie's, pleading for understanding. "I care about you, Marie. I love you, and I want to be with you. I would never intentionally hurt you, but I know my past has caused some issues. I'm working through it because the last thing I want to do is to lose you."

Marie felt tears welling up in her eyes as she listened, her heart softening with every word. Dupree's sincerity was undeniable.

"I cherish what we have," Dupree continued, his voice steady but filled with emotion. "We may not see each other often, but every moment with you feels like magic. I want to protect that, to nurture it. I never want you to feel like you can't trust me or that you're better off without me. Whatever it takes, I'll make it right."

The room was silent, the weight of Dupree's words were hanging heavily in the air. "Marie," Dupree whispered, stepping even closer. "I came back for you. I want you to come with me. Let's go home together."

Marie's breath caught in her throat, and her heart swelled with a mix of surprise and happiness. Slowly, a radiant smile spread across her face, her eyes shining brightly.

Catherine and Tasha watched in awe; their hands clasped together in silent excitement. "Oh my gosh," Tasha whispered, her voice filled with warmth. "This is so beautiful."

Dupree glanced at them, offering a small, grateful smile. "If it's okay with you ladies, I'd like to take Marie with me."

Marie nodded, her voice trembling with emotion. "Okay, you guys, I'm going with Dupree." She turned to her friends, her gratitude evident. "Thank you for everything, for listening, for being here. I can't tell you how much it means to me."

Tasha grinned, her eyes twinkling. "How about that sign, huh?"

Marie laughed, the sound light and joyous. "Won't He do it?"

Catherine chuckled, nodding. "He sure will. God sent that sign just for you."

As Marie and Dupree left, hand in hand, the warmth of their connection radiated through the room. Marie felt a profound sense of peace and fulfillment, believing that only wonderful things lay ahead.

In the car, as they drove away, Marie leaned back with a contented sigh. Her heart was full and her spirit lifted. At that moment, she knew this was just the beginning of something truly special.

Chapter Forty-One

Spend the Night

Dupree turned to Marie and asked softly, "Are you coming with me?"

Marie blinked, caught off guard by the directness of his question. "What?"

"You heard me, Marie. Are you coming with me?"

Marie's heart fluttered at the intensity in his voice. "Do you want me to come with you?"

"You know I do," Dupree replied earnestly, leaning closer. "You heard what I said back there? That was for you. Every word was real. That was the real me, and I know you felt it because you know me, the true me. I want you to come with me."

Marie hesitated, a small smile tugging at the corners of her lips. "I have to go home first. I didn't pack anything, and I've got a flight at nine in the morning. Can you drop me off at the airport by seven?"

Dupree's gaze softened, and he nodded without hesitation. "I'll do anything for you, Marie. Whatever you need, just say the word, and it's done."

Marie smiled, feeling the warmth of Dupree's words seep into her heart. "Okay."

The car ride back to Marie's place was filled with easy conversation, laughter, and the kind of comfortable silence that only comes with deep connection. They talked about everything and nothing, reminiscing about old memories and sharing dreams for the future. Everything felt right again.

At her apartment, Marie quickly packed her suitcase, her excitement barely contained. It wasn't just about the trip, it was about this moment, about them finding their way back to each other. With her bag in hand, she returned to Dupree, who was waiting patiently, his eyes lighting up when he saw her.

The night unfolded like a dream. They spent hours talking, laughing, and rediscovering each other. The weight of the past lifted, replaced by a renewed sense of joy and connection. Every smile, every touch, every word felt like a piece of their story falling perfectly into place.

As they sat on the couch, the city lights casting a soft glow around them, Dupree took Marie's hand in his. "Marie, tonight reminded me of what's truly important. It's you. It's always been you."

Marie's heart swelled, her eyes glistening happily. "I feel the same way. Tonight…it's like we found our way back to where we were always meant to be."

They sat there, wrapped in the warmth of each other's presence, the world outside fading away. In that moment, Marie knew with absolute certainty, Dupree was her person. No matter what the future held, this bond they shared would keep them connected forever.

As the night stretched into the early hours, Marie and Dupree both felt an overwhelming sense of gratitude. After all the ups and downs, they had found their way back to each other, stronger and more certain than ever. Their hearts were full, and their souls at peace.

For Marie and Dupree, this was only the beginning. And as they looked toward the future, hand in hand, they knew their love story was far from over. It was just getting started.

Chapter Forty-Two
Catching Flights and Feelings

Marie woke up at the crack of dawn, her excitement obvious. She didn't want to risk missing her flight. Today was the day she'd see Marcellus, a moment she had long awaited. But as she glanced over at Dupree, still peacefully asleep, a smile spread across her face. Last night had been magical, a night filled with intimacy, intellect, connection, and warmth. Marie felt a wave of gratitude for the rekindled bond between them.

As they drove to the airport, the early morning light casting a soft glow over the city, Marie and Dupree shared quiet moments of laughter and lingering conversation. When they arrived, Dupree parked the car and walked around to open Marie's door. They embraced tightly, their connection unmistakable.

"Thank you for last night," Dupree whispered, his voice laced with sincerity.

Marie smiled, her heart full. "I can't wait to do it all again. Let's keep this going, Dupree."

Dupree nodded, placing a gentle kiss on Marie's lips. "We will. Safe travels, Marie."

As Marie boarded her flight, the exhaustion from the night before caught up with her, and she drifted off to sleep. The flight was a brief escape, a moment to recharge before the whirlwind ahead.

Chapter Forty-Three
Superbowl Night

Marcellus had called early that morning, leaving Marie a message with all the details, her hotel, the game, everything. When Marie arrived at the Hilton in New Orleans, Louisiana she was awestruck by its beauty and proximity to the Louisiana Superdome. Excitement buzzed through her as she prepared for the big game.

The Superdome was electric. Fans filled the stands, their cheers echoing through the air. Marcellus, the star quarterback, was in his element. He commanded the field with precision, reading the defense, making split-second decisions, and throwing passes with unparalleled accuracy. Every play was a testament to his skill and leadership. He threw for over 350 yards, leading his team to victory. The Steelers won the Super Bowl again, and the crowd erupted in celebration.

As the festivities wound down and the adrenaline of the game faded, Marie finally got the chance to see Marcellus. It was well past midnight, but the moment was worth the wait. They embraced tightly, the months apart melting away in an instant. Their laughter and shared stories filled the quiet spaces between them as they reveled in each other's presence.

"Marie," Marcellus said, looking deeply into her eyes, "I've missed you so much."

Marie smiled, her heart swelling with happiness. "I've missed you too. It's been too long."

They decided to extend the night, heading to Bourbon Street for a late-night meal. The city was alive, and they walked hand in hand, stealing kisses and soaking in the magic of the moment. They talked about everything, the game, their lives, their dreams, and each word drew them closer.

After their meal, they strolled through the streets, enjoying the cool night air and each other's company. The connection between them felt effortless, as if no time had passed at all. Eventually, they returned to the Hilton, where the night continued in a swirl of love and intimacy.

For Marie and Marcellus, this was more than a reunion, it was a reaffirmation of their bond. In each other's arms, they found a sense of peace and belonging. The love they shared, though tested by time and distance, remained unshaken.

As they lay together, the world outside quiet and still, Marie felt an overwhelming sense of joy. This was where she was meant to be, in the arms of the man who made her feel alive. Marcellus was her person, her home. And in that moment, as they drifted off to sleep, they knew they had found something truly special.

Chapter Forty-Four

The Finale

The night had been magical. As Marie watched Marcellus wave her off into the luxury shuttle, she felt like she was floating on air. He had made her feel like royalty, and for the first time, she believed she was truly the one. Every glance, every word, every touch whispered that she was his queen. The world could wait because, for one night, it revolved around them.

Marie, on her way to the airport, couldn't shake the smile off her face. Even as she settled in at her gate, ready to head back to Nebraska, she felt the warmth of Marcellus' embrace still lingering. Her perfect getaway was ending, but her heart was still dancing in New Orleans.

Then it happened. Through the terminal's crowd, she spotted him, Marcellus, but he wasn't alone. Walking toward the adjacent gate, Vanessa clung to his arm, with a radiant smile on her face. They were with other team members and their partners, laughing and chatting. But Vanessa, catching sight of Marie, suddenly tightened her grip on Marcellus and pulled him aside.

"Hey, walk with me for a sec," Vanessa murmured, her voice deceptively sweet. Marcellus, oblivious to the brewing storm, followed without hesitation.

As they approached, Marie felt her heart skip a beat. She tried to play it cool, but inside, she was unraveling.

"Don't I know you?" Vanessa asked, her tone dripping with fake curiosity.

Marie chuckled, trying to keep the atmosphere light. "Yeah, Vanessa, right? We've crossed paths."

Vanessa tilted her head, her eyes narrowing. "Funny, isn't it? Both of us in New Orleans at the same time. Small world."

"New Orleans is a big city," Marie replied calmly, refusing to break under the pressure. "Lots of people visit."

Marcellus, sensing the tension, tried to intervene. "Hey, what's going on? Marie, how've you been? Vanessa quit playing let's go!"

Marie's eyes locked with his. "Just catching a flight home, Marcellus. That's all."

Vanessa wasn't buying it. "We are going to go, but you know, Marcellus, last night you told me you needed some space to celebrate with the team. You said you guys wanted to keep it low-key. And you kept it low-key all night long huh? But here we are, and look who I find at the airport. It's just crazy!"

Marcellus shifted uncomfortably. "Vanessa, please. You're making this bigger than it is."

"Oh, I'm sure it's nothing," Vanessa sneered, the sarcasm in her voice undeniable. "But it's funny how you always find time for a little extra company."

Marie clenched her fists, fighting to keep her composure. "Look, Vanessa, I'm not here to cause a scene. I'm just waiting for my flight."

Vanessa's eyes flashed with suspicion. "Of course you are. Just a coincidence, right?"

Marcellus stepped in, his voice firm. "Vanessa, let's go. There's nothing here."

As they walked away, Vanessa shot one last glance over her shoulder, her mind racing with doubts and suspicions. She cracked a devious smile like this is my man, just to piss Marie off. Marie watched them go, her heart heavy and her mind clouded with confusion.

The perfect evening and morning had shattered into a million pieces, leaving Marie to pick up the fragments of her heart. She had believed in Marcellus and the dream he had painted for her. But now, reality was sinking in, and it was cold and unforgiving.

As she boarded her flight, Marie vowed to take time to reflect. This wasn't over. She needed to regroup, find clarity, and decide what was next.

But one thing was certain, this was far from the end of her story with Marcellus. The tangled web of emotions, secrets, and lies was just beginning to unravel.

Chapter Forty-Five

The Final Chapter

Marie sank into her seat on the plane, the ache in her chest deepening with each passing moment. The events of the past few hours played over in her mind, leaving her stunned. She had believed, truly believed, that something profound had sparked between her and Marcellus. The way he looked at her, the way he made her feel like she was the only woman in the world, had filled her with a rare, intoxicating hope. But now, staring blankly at the seat in front of her, Marie could feel that hope slipping away, replaced by a cold, stark reality.

Marcellus was still with Vanessa. The thought pierced Marie like a dagger. What was she to him, really? A fleeting distraction? A monetary escape? Marie's heart screamed betrayal, but her mind, sharp and ever-practical, forced her to confront the truth.

With a deep breath, Marie squared her shoulders, her resolve hardening. Life had a way of teaching harsh lessons, and this was just another one to add to the list. She reminded herself of the wisdom her parents had imparted into her growing up about love, about relationships, and about the games people play. "This is life," Marie whispered to herself. "People come and go. They love, they lie, they play."

Marie was no stranger to heartache, but she knew better than to let it consume her. Instead, she would learn from it. She understood now that it wasn't just about the pain, it was about how you handled it, how you moved forward. "If it makes you happy, keep it. If it makes you sad, let it go. If it makes you mad, let it go." Her mother's words echoed in her mind, a soothing balm to her wounded heart.

As the plane lifted off, Marie looked out the window, the world beneath her growing smaller. She made a silent vow to herself. She wouldn't let this break her. She wouldn't let anyone, not Marcellus, not Vanessa, or anyone else define her worth. She had her own life, her own goals, her own dreams. And if anyone thought they could toy with her emotions without consequence, they had another thing coming.

Marie smiled faintly, a glimmer of her old confidence returning. "They'll learn," she thought. "I'll make sure they do. I know who I am. And I'm not done yet."

This wasn't the end of her story—far from it. It was merely a chapter closing, with a new one on the horizon. Marie knew her worth, and she knew that in the end, she would rise above it all. Her journey was just beginning, and she was ready for whatever came next.

To be continued…

End of Book 1

Stay tuned for Love, Lessons, Lies,

and the Game of Life Book 2,

where the secrets deepen, the stakes rise,

and the drama takes an unexpected turn.

Will Marie find her truth?

Will Vanessa uncover the lies?

And where does Marcellus' heart truly lie?

What about Dupree?

The answers await…

We really appreciate you taking time out to read,

Love, Lessons, Lies, and the Game of Life Book 1

The Beginning

Please do a review on Amazon.com

to let us know what you think.

Dr. Charmaine Marie is an accomplished author, educator, and enhanced life skills coach dedicated to empowering individuals of all ages. With a passion for personal development, she has authored numerous best-selling books, including the My Daddy's Baby family drama series, I Am Unstoppable, I Am Beautiful, and How Do You Love Yourself Unconditionally? Her work spans across genres, offering drama, inspiration, self-love, and practical guidance. As a devoted advocate for youth empowerment, Dr. Charmaine also created the Success At Its Best: Enhanced Life Skills Curriculum and Workbook to equip young minds with essential life skills. Through her writing, she aims to inspire readers to be their best self, embrace their full potential, live authentically, and pursue their dreams with confidence.

www.ingramcontent.com/pod-product-compliance
Lightning Source LLC
Chambersburg PA
CBHW060425260626
47161CB00005B/1787